TERI WOODS PUBLISHING PRESENTS

NY'S FINEST

Masquerade

BY SAM BLACK

Published by Teri Woods Publishing

Published by Teri Woods Publishing

TERI WOODS PUBLISHING PRESENTS

NY'S FINEST

Masquerade

BY SAM BLACK

Published by Teri Woods Publishing

Note:
Sale of this book without a front cover may be unauthorized. If this book is purchased without a cover it may be reported to the publisher as "unsold or destroyed." Neither the author nor the publisher may receive payment for the sale of this book.

This novel is a work of fiction.   Any resemblance to real people, living or dead, actual events, establishments, organizations, and/or locales are intended to give it a sense of reality and authenticity. Other names, characters, places and incidents are either products of the author's imagination or are used fictitiously, as are those fictionalized events and incidents that involve real persons and did not occur or are set in the future.

Published by:
TERI WOODS PUBLISHING
P.O. Box 20069
New York, NY 10001-0005
www.teriwoodspublishing.com

ISBN: 0-9773234-6-3
Copyright: Processing
Library of Congress Catalog Card No: Processing

Masquerade Credits
Story Written by Sam Black for Teri Woods Publishing
Edited by Teri Woods and Jessica Tyler for Teri Woods Publishing
Text Formation by Teri Woods for Teri Woods Publishing
Cover Concept by Teri Woods for Teri Woods Publishing

Printed in Canada

Published by Teri Woods Publishing

Dedication

This book is dedicated to New York City, the greatest city in the world. You made me on the streets of 1, 2, 5th and you made my life the best it could ever be! I love you, New York City.

Thank You's

I can only thank YOU, whoever YOU are reading this. In the beginning all I ever asked for, was for someone to read me. I thank you for your support of my company and the books my company publishes, without YOU there could be no me and no movement for young, black, independent writers. I want to thank Sam Black for coming home. Whatever force brought you into my life, I'm grateful for you and the work we have accomplished over the years. You deserve the glory, you are an amazing writer. To sum it up best, if I were a lighter, you would be my spark and together we make fires. I love you dearly, I always have from the beginning and I am truly humbled for being a part of all the history that we have made together. I want to thank my family for always being there, my mom for everything, my step-dad, Carol, my brothers, Dex, Chuck, Carl, my sister, Brenda, my daughter, Gypsy Girl Jessie where are you Jessie? To my boys Lukie Baby and Brandy B (aka Can't Sit Down and Can't Listen) you keep me on track fellas, if nothing else and you love your mommy. I love you my little family and I thank you for keeping me on track and to the men and women in my life that I have the pleasure of interacting with, you keep my circle of life the best to be in. Thank you everybody so much, I love you and I love you and I love you!

October 30, 2010
9:00 P.M.

"Don't move! Don't you fucking move! Get out of the car now!"

The driver of the burgundy MPV looked at the passenger. Everything had happened too fast for his mind to react. One minute ago, they had been driving along Vernon Boulevard, the sounds of Biggie providing the rhythm as they rode. Next thing they were being cut off by a blue Crown Victoria with blue lights flashing in their grill, forcing them to skid across the street nose first into the entrance of a chemical plant parking lot.

"What the fuck is going on?" asked the passenger already knowing what he and his partner were holding inside the car. He gripped his gun in his right hand, tipped off the safety with his thumb, ready to blast. And as soon as he was about to, he realized that they weren't being robbed, but worse... *It's a fucking detective's car?* He cursed to himself and lowered the gun back down to his lap.

"Fuck we gonna do?!" he hissed to the driver, as the detectives jumped out of the car.

"Just chill," the driver said, gripping the steering wheel. His first thought was to hit reverse and make a break for it, but the way the female detective had her gun trained on him, he knew the attempt would be futile. This was the NYPD, he already knew they shoot to kill and he wasn't about to take the chance.

The other detective, a tall lanky Black dude, had his gun aimed over the roof of the Crown Vic and had steady eye contact with the passenger of the MPV, his eyes mockingly daring him to move. He slowly came around the trunk of the car, gun held with both hands, his left cupping his right, as he slowly approached the driver's side.

The female was a lot more gung-ho. She was half way out the car before it skipped to a complete stop. She had the complete uniform including police cap and knee high black shiny riding boots. Her long mane of autumn brown hair was pulled in a pony tail, but still flowed down her back, bouncing with the fluidity of her movements as she eased up on the passenger side of the vehicle, her gun aimed at the passenger's head.

"Turn off the car and toss the keys out the window!" her partner ordered.

A few cars drove by, but seeing the guns aimed and ready, made them only drive by faster.

"Is there a problem, officer?" the driver asked calmly and simply asked as he carefully complied with the demand, reaching slowly toward the gear shit as he looked at the cop pointing the gun for his head.

"Just do it!" the male detective barked.

The keys hit the ground with a jingle.

"Now reach out and open the door from the outside...slowly," the male detective instructed.

"Passenger, you too!" the female detective added, angling herself for a clean sight line.

Both driver and passenger did as they were told. The passenger kicked the gun as far as he could under the seat as he got out, hands raised.

"Yo, man, what y'all stop..."

2

That was the last word the passenger got out, before the female detective fired three quick shots. The first hit him in the throat and went straight through the back of his neck, coating the inside of the MPV with warm blood and tissue. The second and third shots hit him execution style in the head and his heart. His body slumped over the open door then gravity pulled him to the pavement.

"What the fuck? You-you killed my man!"

The driver screamed in anguish and confusion as it hit him in the face like a ton of bricks. *They're not even cops.* Then, the whole picture opened up to him, it was a set up.

"Y'all ain't no fuckin' police!"

"We never said we were," she giggled, rounding the car as her accomplice put two in the driver's face. The impact blew him back into the driver's seat, bent double in a grotesque position of death, just as a dark brown Buick hooptie pulled up. Inside the hooptie were three men, all jumped out the Buick, one carrying a duffle bag, and quickly got in the MPV, throwing the deceased driver to the pavement. The driver of the Crown Vic got in the car with them. The other female officer, got in the Buick, skidded off in one direction as the MPV headed in another, leaving two helpless bodies leaking blood into the concrete.

Several minutes later, the MPV pulled up into the parking lot of the Jade East Motel on North Conduit Avenue. It was a seedy motel that catered to prostitutes, tricks and dope fiends. There were only a few cars in the parking lot of the open faced motel. An old rusty Nissan on one end, a grey Bronco with Jersey plates a few spaces down and a yellow '92 Mazda RX7 parked in front of the office. The MPV pulled up beside the RX7 and killed the engine.

The four men in the MPV checked and double-checked their weapons. No one spoke and no music played as they mentally prepared them selves for the task at hand. Bop, Face, Mellow and Tank were no strangers to the stickup game. Coming up in Brownsville, they had mastered the trade early in life, so there was never any amateurish mistakes. In this case, all were well aware of what was about to go down. But they were also aware that this wasn't just a robbery. This would be an all out massacre. Usually in a stickup, if a robbery became a homicide, it's a problem, something went wrong. But this would not be that and this time it was different. Everybody in the room had to die, that was their instructions. But it was worth a bunch of dead bodies. Seven hundred and Fifty stacks were worth a lot of dead bodies. On top of the seven fifty, there were six kilos of pure heroin somewhere in the MPV. It was in a hydraulic stash somewhere hid. They didn't know how to get it, but they knew a nigga who did. It was for that person they had agreed to do this hit for the seven fifty.

"Ya'll niggas ready?" Face asked from the front passenger seat. At nineteen, he was next to the youngest in the crew. But he was its de facto leader. His wiry build and average height weren't impressive. However, it masked a temperament that was pure dynamite. Face was by far the wildest. But he was also a planner which made him doubly dangerous and effective.

Tank cocked back the Mac-10 and sneered, "Naw, is them niggas ready?"

"Yo Tank, I'm dead ass," Face turned around, looked at Tank in the seat behind him. "These niggas ain't playin' no games. They smell a cross and shit gon' get ugly real fast. And if one of 'em live and find out it was us...." Face shook his head. "You gonna see what real beef is."

"That's why we ain't gonna give 'em a chance to smell nothin' but gun smoke," Mellow confirmed, in his laid back style.

Face nodded, then added, "Exactly, so everybody stick

to the plan. We bust the door and we start blazin'. And remember..."

"Nobody lives," Tank finished for him in an aggravated tone. "Nig-ga, I got it! Now, are we gon' talk about it or be about it?!"

Face knew that Tank's adrenalin was intoxicating his blood stream, so he let his tone slide. Instead, he answered by holding up the twin Glock-45 he was gripping. He looked at Bop in the driver's seat. Bop was the wheel man of the crew and had also been the driver of the Crown Victoria.

"Bop, be on point," said Face knowing his team put in work.

"Always, my nigga," Bop smiled, giving Face dap, a slight nod of the head.

Face, Mellow and Tank got out, tucking their weapons. Tank grabbed the duffle bag he had brought as a decoy, because the occupants of the motel room they were visiting were expecting a delivery.

As they slowly entered the motel's small office, they heard the sounds of a television coming from the back room. The door behind the counter opened as Antoinette peeked around it before stepping to the counter.

"Took you long enough," she quipped with a smirk.

Face hit her with the dimples that made her pussy twitch. "Did you handle your business?"

"Room 232, at the top of the stairs."

"How many?"

"Three niggas, two bitches"

Face nodded letting her know she did good, then he and his crew walked out. As soon as they did, Antoinette left out behind them, taking one last look at the blood that was beginning to seep from under the back door.

Face and his crew headed for the stairs while Antoinette headed for the RX7 in the parking lot. As she was about to get in, a bone skinny, light skin chick in a halter and mini skirt came out of a motel room.

"You straight?" she asked, scratching her neck and licking her ashy lips.

Antoinette eyed her with disgust. Dope fiend hoe was written all over her face.

"Naw, yo," Antoinette replied, opening the RX7's door.

"Can I get a ride to Farmers?"

Bitch you can't get nothing, Antoinette sucked her teeth and answered her question by slamming the door in the dope fiend's face. She pulled off just as she heard the first shots ring out from inside the motel and break the stillness of the night. She floored the RX7 and disappeared on North Conduit.

Face and his crew had climbed the single flight to the second floor cautiously. The cold October air swirled around them. In the distance, they heard glass breaking and car alarms wailing. Face smiled to himself, remembering that it was Mischeif Night, the night before Halloween, that in every hood, the devious used it as an excuse to be at their devilish best. Face remembered his childhood antics when he was younger. As he knocked on the door, ready to do his own devilments, Mellow kept going walking to the end of the breezeway and positioned himself. His job was to make sure no one came out of any room and pinned Face and Tank inside.

An Asian chick peeked out the curtain, and then disappeared. A second later, a fat brown dude peeked out. Face nodded subtly and so did the dude. When Face saw the Dude's eyes fall on the duffle bag Tank was carrying, he knew they were in. Tank had the Mac-10 concealed behind the duffle bag. As soon as the door opened, they went into action. Tank slung the duffle bag in the fat dude's face, catching him off guard as Face quickly fired three shots into his chest. Boom! Boom! Boom!

Before the fat dude hit the floor, Face put the gun in

his right hand to the Asian chick's screaming head and the gun in his left to some Spanish chick's sobbing temple, and splattered them simultaneously.

"Where's the money?!" Tank barked at another dude holding his gun to his head. The dude was a short, muscular bull of a man, almost as bullish as Tank.

Seeing that the gunmen didn't wear masks and had killed his man from jump, the dude knew he was about to die.

"Nigga, suck my dick," he hissed, eying Tank hard.

"I got it," Face exclaimed, snatching a bulky duffle bag from under the bed.

Tank put his gun under the dude's chin and blew his brains all over the wall and the ceiling.

"That's four," said Tank

"It's supposed to be five," Face remarked, looking around frantically.

"What?" Tank yelled his ears still ringing from the explosion of gun fire. He was so amped up he had forgotten all about Antoinette's info. They didn't have long to wait. They had to get what they came for and get the hell out of there.

"Down," Face yelled, snatching Tank to the floor right before automatic gunfire erupted and whizzed over their heads.

Face saw the gun nozzle sticking out the bathroom door a split second before it spit with murderous intent. He and Tank, half covered by the bed, returned fire, trying to shoot through the wall into the bathroom.

"Aaaaargggghh!" Tank bellowed as he sprayed round after round until the wall and the door of the bathroom looked like Swiss cheese. Then the gun went silent when it clicked on empty.

"Let's go," Face ordered.

Mentally, he was shaking his head at Tank. You never

empty your clip in a shoot out if you can help it. Face had emptied one Glock but he knew he still had a few rounds left in his other. Always save something for the get away.

Tank and Face scrambled for the door, as another burst of automatic gunfire blazed the room, blowing chunks out of the wall and door frame. Face, with the duffle bag in one hand and the gun in the other, took the stairs three at a time, with Tank right on his heels. They would've been dead if it wasn't for Mellow. The stairs went right under the trajectory of the room, so all the gunman had to do was stand in the door and pick them off. Thanks to Mellow, that didn't happen. He opened fire on the front plate glass window of the room, effectively cutting the gunman off from the door and allowing Tank and Face to make it to the MPV.

Mellow jumped the second floor railing and landed squarely on his feet, then scampered to the MPV. The gunman, an authentically built Dred, came out reloading his Callico then blazed the MPV as it skidded out of the parking lot. The Dred hopped the railing like Mellow and took off on foot behind the MPV, the Callico spitting shells like sunflower seeds. He managed to blow out the back window and the rear left tire, but to no avail. The MPV screeched on to North Conduit, cutting off a taxi and a station wagon, and made its getaway.

Just as the MPV was heading southbound, a police cruiser was headed northbound. They saw the flame of the Callico muzzle and the crackle of gunfire in the air. They skidded hard into the parking lot.

"Shit!" Dred cursed, then turned to run.

The passenger cop jumped out.

"Freeze!"

Dred ignored the command. All he heard was boom! Then his left leg went out from under him, and blood gushed from his calf. He fell face first to the pavement.

"Bum-bah-clod!" Dred yelled in anguish as the cop

put his knee in his back and his gun to his head.

"Don't fucking move," the cop hissed, cuffing Dred high and tight.

October 30, 2010
10:00 P.M.

"You sure you ain't hungry? Mischief Night's always a busy night," Detective Rahjohn Griffin asked, offering his partner Natasha Bagley a free meal.

She sucked her teeth and looked away.

"Okay, don't say I didn't warn you," he replied with a shrug, as he turned to the McDonald's drive through receiver. "Let me get the number two and two large Pepsis."

"Diet Pepsi."

"Huh?"

"Diet Pepsi," Natasha repeated with an attitude.

Rahjohn smiled to himself.

"Make that one Pepsi and one Diet Pepsi."

"That'll be $7.78, sir. Please drive thru," a woman's voice could be heard through the large menu display board box.

"Yeah, sure thing," Rahjohn said as he sat back and waited in the drive-thru line. The police radio periodically sounded off in the background. Natasha silently studied his profile out of the corner of her eye.

I hate you Rahjohn Griffin. You make me sick and how dare you have nothing more to offer me than McDonalds. I really can't stand this man. He really makes me sick, she sat thinking to herself. She was a woman that was used to being in control, but somehow this weasel named Rahjohn Griffin had a magical power that took over her and always made her lose her own self-control, not to mention lose the lock she had on her feelings. Only he had the power to make her stomach quiver or her blood boil with a simple gesture. He had the power to drive her crazy.

"So you just gonna sit there?" she huffed. "Act like shit is all good?"

Rahjohn glanced over at her.

It ain't? He asked himself looking at her wondering what the problem was

"Is it?" she shot back asking the question again already knowing it wasn't.

Rahjohn sighed. He knew sexing his partner would be a mistake. *Why did I fuck my partner? Why?* His best friend Gee had told him not to, but of course, Rahjohn Wilson Griffin better known as John John, sometimes simply called John, simply wouldn't listen. How could he listen to any voice of reason?

Detective Natasha Bagley was the baddest lady officer in the 17th Homicide Division, hell, maybe even the NYPD period. If Lil' Wayne wasn't talking about her, then who was he talking about? She was 5'9" and a succulent golden Crown that reminded him of Egyptian gold. Her chunky light brown eyes and small upturned nose gave her a smoky, sexy cover girl look. She wasn't ghetto thick, but her body was toned like a track star.

"Come on Tash, don't act like that. You're the one who said that it's not. Not me, I never said that," he added.

Natasha eyed him for a minute, then folded her arms across her chest.

"Where is this going, Rahjohn?" she asked calling him by his government. And don't you dare say, 'what do you mean by this' because you know damn well what I'm talking about.

The line moved up a car length.

I wish we could just listen to the radio. She wouldn't

like it if I suggested that right now at all.

"I mean, what's wrong with the way it is now?" John hedged.

"You mean, just fucking, right? Casual sex and no commitment," she probed as if he must be retarded.

"Friends with benefits," he smiled coyly.

"Friends with benefits," she repeated, testing the words on her lips. "So it's cool, if I see other people?"

She was trying to arouse his jealousy, but it backfired when he answered, "Sure, no problem, why not?"

"Damn, just put me on the corner," she huffed, turning away from the conversation.

Rahjohn was use to this scenario with women. He was thirty-two years old, no kids and he was what all women in the world would describe as sinfully fine. He had brown cocoa skin, curly black hair that made people think he was Dominican and greenish hazel eyes that could melt the heart of the coldest women when he used them to seduce.

He was dedicated to his daily work out sessions that kept him in the shape of a boxer, weighing in at one hundred and eighty pounds and standing six feet even. Rahjohn was the consummate ladies man. Born and raised in Harlem, he was undeniably Mr. Swag, and obviously he was far from a thug, even though he was born and bred in the hood. Being a cop was his life's dream. He grew up hating the way white cops came into Harlem and treated Black people like animals and illiterates. At the same time, he despised the way the neighborhood thugs blatantly disrespected the elders and terrorized the community. He made it his business to take it to the racist cops and the street's corrupt with equal force.

Rahjohn was a solid Black man, but when it came to women, he was a floater, a rolling stone and he was extremely allergic to any commitment that lasted longer than the morning after. Natasha cursed herself for even getting involved with the notorious precinct playboy. He had already run through most of the attractive women at the precinct, and she knew it. But she too couldn't resist. At first, it was mutually understood that it was just a fling between two mutually, consenting, adults. And somewhere along the way, her feelings got involved. And now, more was at stake than just her feelings.

She started to tell him what she really needed to get off her chest, but before she could, the dispatcher came over the radio.

"Ten-ten, Dispatch to Charlie Six."

Rahjohn picked up the handheld and answered, "Charlie six, go ahead."

"I've got a report of shots fired at 1637 North Conduit Avenue..." He cut her off.

"The Jade East Motel?"

"Affirmative. Several victims, all likely," the dispatcher squawked, using the term 'likely' which meant likely a goner.

"Copy that. Charlie Six en route," Rahjohn confirmed.

He inched back, blowing the horn for the car behind him to let him out, then pulled out, commenting wistfully, "Damn, I'm starving."

A few traffic lights and several minutes later, he pulled into the Jade East parking lot. The flashing blue and red lights of the several police cruisers and the ambulance always reminded him of some kind of macabre carnival. The crime scene investigators, EMT and the press scurried back and forth, while beyond the yellow tape, onlookers gawked at the spectacle of death.

Rahjohn and Natasha approached the sergeant who was in charge of the crime scene. He was a heavyset guy with a bald head and thick mustache.

"Well, I guess spending my day tomorrow trick or treating is out, huh Frank?" Rahjohn cracked, shaking the sergeant's hand.

"Well, you can still go through the house of horrors,"

the sergeant replied, referring to the open motel door. "You got four victims, two male, two female, real messy. We've got one, Lombardi took him down. He ain't sayin' shit though."

"One of the shooters?" Rahjohn quizzed, expectantly.

"I wish... looks more like an intended victim."

Rahjohn nodded as all three headed upstairs to the room. Inside, the crime scene investigators busied themselves taking pictures, dusting for prints and searching for slugs and spent cartridges. The broken glass crunched under their shoes as they entered the room.

Natasha had seen scenes like this a thousand times, but death was something she'd never get used to. It always reminded her of her own mortality and disgusted her with the evil that men do.

The two females both laid on their sides, the Asian girl's eyes still open in an expression of the final horror. A fat dude was slumped between them, his brains soaking into the carpet and the bedspread. The other male on the bed, leaned against the raggedy head board, half his head exploded and his thoughts still dripping off the ceiling in crimson streaks.

"From what we can tell, looks like an ambush," the sergeant explained, pointing to the doorway. "No signs of forced entry and neither guy had a chance to pull their weapons, even though they were both armed."

Rahjohn could see the pistol stuck in the waist of the dead man's jeans. Rahjohn ruled out robbery as a motive, seeing that both men had on diamond encrusted watches and platinum jewelry. In his mind, this was definitely a hit.

The sergeant began to move around the room, recreating the crime.

"I'd say it was at least two of them, too much damage for one guy unless we're lookin' for Rambo," the sergeant chuckled. "So they come in blasting, hit whoever answered the door then dropped the other two over here next to the

14

hallway. Someone runs up on victim number four on the bed and whacks him point blank."

Rahjohn pointed to the wall that fronted the bathroom. It was so full of holes you could see light seeping through from the bathroom, and the shadow of someone moving around in there.

"If everything was so clean, why all the fire power?" he asked.

"I was getting to that," the sergeant answered. "There was a third man, probably the guy we collared, in the bathroom when the shooters came in."

"Lucky guy," Natasha quipped.

"Depends on what side of the fence you're standing on. So they pinned the guy in the bathroom once he made his presence known then made their getaway."

"There was another shooter outside the room," Natasha remarked, gesturing to the glass on the floor. "Someone had to be shooting from the outside. Look, the glass is all inside the room. So the other shooter waited outside, kept the ones inside covered as they got away."

The sergeant nodded.

"How'd I miss that? I must really be getting old," he joked already figuring this scene out before they got there.

"Where's the perp now?" Rahjohn asked.

"St. Luke's," the sergeant answered.

"He gonna make it?" Rahjohn inquired knowing how his people went in.

"No reason why he shouldn't, he was hit in the leg."

Rahjohn scanned the room once more.

"Are there any witnesses? Doesn't this place have a surveillance system?"

"Yes and yes," was the sergeant's reply. "Some female says she saw a woman leaving the office right as the shooting began."

"Leaving the office? What's that have to do with this?"

Rahjohn asked.

"You haven't seen the office yet."

Her face looked angelic, almost like she was sleeping. The color of brown cinnamon, with long luscious eyelashes, full pouty lips and a slit throat, through which her life seeped out on to the dirty tile floor. Rahjohn kneeled down beside her, examining her throat.

"This cut looks almost surgical. Pretty girl, who is she?"

"Renee Owens. She was the manager on duty," the sergeant informed him, shaking his head. "She was only nineteen years old."

Rahjohn could hear the anguish in the sergeant's voice. He knew the sergeant had a daughter about the same age. Rahjohn stood up.

"Where's the witness?" he asked.

"We took her down to the precinct to take her statement."

"What about the tape?"

The sergeant beckoned for them to follow him deeper into the back room. "At first we thought the perps had taken the tape because we found the recorder empty, but....," the sergeant explained as he moved several books aside that sat on a lone shelf. Behind it was a compartment that housed a VCR. "The owner told us that he'd been robbed so much, and every time, the perp would take the tape. So he decided to setup a backup."

"Smart man," Natasha remarked.

"And lucky for us," Rahjohn added.

The sergeant pressed play then rewound the tape. They watched as everything played backward in blurry super speed. The sergeant didn't stop until the night manager pulled up in the grey Bronco.

"This was about five o'clock when she arrived," said the sergeant.

Rahjohn and Natasha watched Antoinette pull up in the RX7, look around, then head inside the office, where she disappeared from view.

"Too bad the guy didn't have a camera in his office too," Natasha said.

They fast forwarded the tape watching the sun set in seconds. Then after several minutes of accelerated nothingness, an MPV pulled in the lot and parked.

"This is when it gets interesting," the sergeant commented.

As they watched Face, Tank and Mellow go in and out the office then head for the stairs, a uniformed officer rushed into the room.

"Detective Griffin."

Rahjohn turned his attention to the officer.

"Yeah?"

"The captain's over on Vernon Boulevard. He wants you over there, pronto!"

October 30, 2010
10:00 P.M.

"Where you been?" Baby Wise asked, never taking his eyes off the Giants – Cowboy's game playing on the big screen.

Vita slowly shut the door of the one and a half million dollar home she shared with Baby Wise in Jamaica Estates, Queens' prestigious gated community,

"I had to.... I just needed to clear my mind," she stammered, anxious to cover up her actual whereabouts.

After she had abandoned the brown Buick, she had quickly stripped herself of the mechanic's jumper suit she wore in the hit. She then burned everything. The jumper, the car and the autumn colored wig and pony tail in a deserted section of Brooklyn. Vita then got into her '98 powder blue Mercedes Benz jeep and headed home. She was hoping Wise wouldn't be there, but he was and he had been waiting for her.

The game went to a commercial. Wise stood slowly, eyeing Vita coldly.

"Come here," he commanded.

"Please Wise, I-I wasn't out long.... I..."

"Come here," he repeated, his voice just above a menacing whisper.

Slowly, Vita crossed the heated hardwood floor as her high heel Gucci sling backs cracked against the floor in a broken rhythm of apprehension. She stood before Baby Wise, her head down and hands clasped in front of her, like a child anticipating punishment.

18

Baby Wise gently cupped her chin and lifted her head to look in her eyes.

"Now... I'm gonna ask you again, and this time... don't lie to me", he warned then added, "Where were you?"

A solitary tear welled in her left eye.

"Baby...Baby Wise; I swear I'm not lying to you. I...I needed to clear my head. I went to the mall and....I"

Smack!

He backhanded her so quick she didn't realize she was on the floor, dizzy, looking up at him.

"You gonna tell me," Baby Wise seethed, still not raising his voice, which actually was a bad sign, a very bad sign. Vita knew that when he yelled, the beatings weren't as bad. He took off his alligator skin belt.

"Wise, please," Vita sobbed, trying to scoot away.

"Tell me where you was at!"

"The mall, baby, I swear."

"Tell me!" He growled this time.

"Wise, nooooooo," Vita screamed, holding up her hand in a weak attempt to fend off the blows.

He rained blows on her incessantly. Vita howled and writhed in pain.

"I'm sorry, baby, please stop!" she begged, turning over and trying to get to her feet, but Baby Wise snatched her up by her right ankle and commenced to beat her like a Hebrew slave.

"Who was you wit', huh?! Who?!" Baby Wise hissed, punctuating every blow with a stinging question mark.

"Nobody, I swear," Vita screamed.

It wasn't only the beatings that were a stable in the relationship; so were the accusations. Baby Wise gave her anything and everything she wanted. On top of that, he was the rare dude that never strayed when it came to other women. He was totally committed to Vita. But when it came to thinking about Vita being with someone else, he would get violently jealous. She had even woken up one night gasping for air. Wise was choking her in her sleep all because he dreamed she had cheated on him. She walked with his finger prints around her neck for weeks all because of a dream.

Vita was no stranger to putting in work. But when it came to Baby Wise, she couldn't kill him, at least not yet. She was ready to put an end to the abuse, but this one she'd take for the team.

The ringing of the door bell was the only thing that saved Vita's ass.

"Who the fuck is it?!" Baby Wise barked, knowing it couldn't be too many people, because very few knew where he rested his head.

"It's Kane, Dunn. Open up!"

Baby Wise looked down at Vita, chest heaving.

"Get up," he said just as calm as spring.

The belt buckle had cut welts on her arms and neck. She winced with pain, as she struggled to her feet. Baby Wise grabbed her by her hair and snatched her to her feet.

"Now get the fuck outta my face," he seethed, shoving her away with so much force, she stumbled and fell to her hands and knees. Using the couch for support, she got back to her feet and stared daggers at Baby Wise's back as she headed up the stairs.

Baby Wise opened the door. Kane and Grip stepped in, shutting the door behind them.

"That bitch ass nigga fucked us, Dunn!" Kane announced with venom in his voice and murder in his eyes.

"Who?" Wise replied in a confused grunt.

"Bacardi, yo, he fucked us! That bitch ass nigga killed Goo and Jay and robbed us!" Kane explained with animated hand gestures.

Baby Wise looked at him with a scowl, trying to wrap his mind around Kane's words.

"Bacardi?" he said, more to himself than to Kane and

Grip, his mind scrambling at the thought.

Bacardi was his main heroin supplier. They had been doing business a long time, they even hung out sometimes. Why would Bacardi just flip, like that? Rob him, kill his people and get on some grimy shit? The thought that someone who knew him, knew how hard he went, would have the audacity to play him made Baby Wise explode like, "What the fuck, yo?!" He snarled in disbelief, then he looked at Kane, "You sure?"

"Am I sure?! Fuck you mean, Am I sure?! Fuckin' Goo and Jay is fuckin' leakin' all over the fuckin' room, half a mill is gone and this muthafucka the only one who knew how it was goin' down! Of course, I'm fuckin' sure!" Kane barked at Wise.

Kane was the only dude in the world that would get away with talking to Baby Wise like that, the reason being that Kane was the only dude in the world that had Baby Wise's back, one hundred percent.

"That faggot muthafucka," Baby Wise based, punching the door so hard he rattled the glass.

He snatched the phone off the glass coffee table and hit Bacardi's number. When Bacardi answered, Baby Wise bellowed into the receiver, "You bitch ass cocksucka! That's how you wanna play?!"

Bacardi ran his tongue up the length of Autumn's succulent butter-toned leg, beginning at her pedicured toes and ending in a series of gentle kisses along the small of her back. She squirmed and gripped the silk sheets, moaning deliciously. Just the sound of her soft moans made Bacardi ache to be inside her, but he forced himself to take his time, pleasuring her in every way.

The night had begun with dinner at Tao's, then a private showing of Russian sables where he brought her a wrap, a full-length and a quarter-length. Then, it was over to Jersey, to a car dealer that didn't ask any questions when Bacardi dumped a paper bag filled with stacks of money totaling seventy grand and copped Autumn a white four door Porsche with the peanut butter interior. He was pulling out all the stops, but Autumn knew there was an ulterior motive... his guilt.

She knew, but Bacardi didn't know she knew that he had gotten another woman pregnant. This was the second time now in the past three years that they had been together, not that it didn't bother her on some level, but she had long since numbed herself to the treachery of a man's devotion.

Even though she was 'wifey' she looked at herself as a kept woman, someone that enjoyed all the perks of an attentive, if not loyal man. She walled her heart away from the pain and lived only on the surface.

"Hmmm baby, right," Autumn's words got caught in her throat as Bacardi sucked on her clit while curling his fingers inside her pussy, massaging her g-spot.

Her pussy spasmed and gushed all over Bacardi's cheeks and goatee, a milky, creamy white that he didn't hesitate to lick up. His tongue game was superb and he had her pussy on fire, throbbing for a dick down.

Autumn turned her body until she was on top of Bacardi. She straddled him then gripped his thick eight and a half inches, and slid it into her wet pussy. She took it out, then penetrated herself again, repeating it over and over because she loved to feel his thick mushroomed dickhead caressing her walls.

"Come on, baby, leave it in, goddamn," Bacardi gritted, his dick twitching for her tight wetness.

"You wanna fuck this pussy, daddy?" Autumn cooed, allowing herself to slide half his dick in, then sliding it back out.

"Hell yeah, you know I do," Bacardi gushed, gripping

her hips.

"Huh?" She teased him.

Bacardi couldn't take any more. He gripped her ass, spread her cheeks and forced her down on his whole dick.

"Ohh yeah, baby, make me take that dick," she gasped, arching her back to meet his every thrust.

She raked her fingers tantalizingly along his chest and she wound her hips and rode him like a pro.

Their bedroom smelled like a mixture of scented candles and good sex, the sounds of flesh smacking flesh. Feeling his building energy, his thrusts becoming pounds, Autumn worked his dick like a jade egg until Bacardi pushed himself as deep as he could go and exploded deep inside her.

Exhausted, Autumn leaned down while Bacardi kissed and sucked her erect nipples, then tongue-kissed her passionately. Autumn laid her head on his chest.

"You know I love you, right?' Bacardi expressed, basking in the ambiance of the afterglow.

"Yes," Autumn replied, circling his nipple with her finger.

"Soon as shit get right, and I get out of this game, I'ma marry the shit outta you, girl," Bacardi remarked, expressing the intention of his heart.

"I know, baby," she answered, but like Sunshine Anderson, she had heard it all before from Bacardi. It seemed like every time he cheated, he would talk about marrying her, as if subconsciously he was trying to convince himself that he would straighten up with a ring on his finger.

But Autumn knew better. Born and raised in Long Island City, better known as Queensbridge, she knew the games men play. Fair exchange is no robbery, because she played her own game, too. It wasn't that she was disloyal to Bacardi. She just pretended to be oblivious to Bacardi's game, and pretended to swallow his bullshit. She was the type of woman that knew what she wanted and how to get it.

She had all but given up on the concept of love and resigned herself to deal with the real world of convenience.

"You hungry, baby?" Autumn asked, lifting her head and looking into his brown eyes.

"Yeah, for your love," he winked. "But since you asked, I'll take a chicken sandwich."

Autumn kissed his nose, then walked out the room. Bacardi watched her plump heart-shaped ass and low slung hips wiggle out the room. *Damn, I got a good girl.*

He knew Autumn didn't deserve how he carried her, but he was young, rich and fine, so the temptation of all the chicks throwing pussy at him was too much to turn down. So, it was something he thought she had just simply learned to accept.

And just when she was out the room and he was about to turn the channel on the television is when his phone rang. He started not to pick it up, but when he saw it was Baby Wise, he answered it.

"Yo," he said happy to hear from his man.

"You bitch ass cocksucka! That's how you wanna play?!"

Bacardi looked at the phone like shit was oozing out of it. *What the fuck is wrong with him?*

"Baby Wise? Yo, Dunn, this Bacardi. You must have dialed the..."

"Nigga, I know who the fuck I'm talking to! A dead man, muthafucka, a goddamn dead man!" Baby Wise huffed, pacing the floor.

Bacardi sat up in the bed. He had no idea where all this was coming from. He was completely dumbfounded. Baby Wise was his best customer. They had never had any Problems or beef before. He had nothing but love for Baby Wise."

"Yo, calm down, Dunnie. What the fuck are you talkin' about?!" Bacardi inquired still at the point, where he was willing to give Baby Wise the benefit of the doubt.

Baby Wise smiled into the phone.

"Oh, now you wanna play stupid, huh? Okay, nigga, I can show you better than I can tell you!"

Click!

"Yo, Wise! Baby Wise!" Bacardi yelled into the phone. He realized he was gone, and wondered aloud, "What the fuck is wrong with that nigga?"

He tried Baby Wise back, but got sent to voice mail. He then hit his lieutenant, Biz.

"Yo, Biz."

"Yeah."

"What up with that Wise situation? It's taken care of right?" Bacardi questioned.

"I don't know. I'm waiting on Black to hit me now," Biz answered.

Bacardi checked his watch.

"He ain't hit you yet?"

"Naw."

Bacardi hung up. Autumn came back into the room.

"Baby, there's no more chicken. You want me to fix you a steak? What's wrong?" she asked, seeing the expression on his face.

"Nothing," he said, deep in thought. "Where's your phone?"

"In my purse."

"Call this number," he said, clicking through his phone address book.

Autumn got out her phone and dialed the digits Bacardi gave her.

"Block the number," he said.

"I already did," she answered with a wink, letting him know she was on point.

The phone rang several times. Autumn was about to hang up when someone answered.

"Yo," the man said.

Autumn looked at Bacardi for what to say.

"Ask him what up," Bacardi whispered.

"What up, what's good?" she asked.

"It's all good, yo. What up, who this?" Rahjohn asked in his best thug passion voice.

Autumn's instincts told her something wasn't right. She hung up.

"Something ain't right," she informed Bacardi.

"Why, what up?"

Bacardi thought for a moment. Could Jay have gotten busted? Was that what Baby Wise was beefing about? Did he think that Bacardi had got on some rat shit and set him up?

"Call the Jade East and ask for Renee. No, no, never mind."

He called Biz back and told him to go to the Jade East and talk to Renee. Shit didn't seem right.

October 30, 2010
10:45 P.M.

By the time Rahjohn answered the dead man's phone, he had been at the Vernon Boulevard crime scene long enough to know two things. One, that both crime scenes were related, and two, that something serious was erupting on the streets of Queens.

This was no ordinary crime scene. All the big brass was there. Two Captains, a Lieutenant, Internal Affairs, the Chief of Detectives and the Chief of Police were all on hand. They were there to make sure every t was crossed and every i was dotted, because the media was eating up the fact that an unmarked police car had been left at the scene and witnesses were saying the murders had been committed by cops, which meant damage control or it could get real ugly, real fast.

To Rahjohn's trained eye, it wasn't hard to tell that the car wasn't an authentic department-issued vehicle, although someone had went through a lot of trouble to make it appear as such. And the press was running with it. Every network was throwing fuel on the fire by interviewing and giving air to disparate versions of the incident. Women in rollers and toothless men got their claim to fame.

"Yep, and then this lady cop jumped out and blew the

27

passenger away."

"A cop car pulled up and the cops took the red van. I bet its drugs in that van, too."

"Yeah, I said it; it was the PO-LICE!"

It seemed like everywhere Rahjohn looked, a civilian was being interviewed, and not the calm, rational, police officers, captains or police spokesmen. Unfortunately, controversy sells, so who cares if you can get the truth for free.

"Griffin, I know you're already on a case, but this takes priority," the chief of detectives Vernon Wilcox said speaking passionately to Rahjohn as he placed his hand around his back. Chief Wilcox was an older, gray-haired, black man with over forty years of experience under his belt. He was Rahjohn's weight and mentor on the force. "I want the bastards who are throwing dirt on the department like this. You understand?"

Rahjohn nodded being the loyal servant to the law that he was. Truth was he knew the case could become political. The press puts heat on the Mayor, the Mayor passes the buck down from Chief of Police to the Chief of Detectives until the buck stopped with Rahjohn the detective assigned to the case and the one with all the pressure to solve it.

"No problem, Vernon. I'm all over it. Just let me tie a ribbon around the Jade East case for the lucky bastard that takes it over," Rahjohn quipped.

"Whatever you need Griffin, you'll get. Anybody gets in your way, tell me, you understand!"

"Yes, sir."

"I want you all over this until this case is solved and I want it solved now! Internal Affairs is all up my ass, I can't even walk straight," he arched his eyebrows and held up his hands. "You got to get these guys off the streets, you hear me, kid? And I mean now!" Wilcox grumbled before walking away.

Rahjohn and Natasha talked with the officers who were first on the scene, then with a few people who said they saw the situation go down. Then they came back together to compare notes.

"Told you it'll be a busy night," he quipped.

"Goes with the territory," Natasha replied.

"Okay," Rahjohn began, looking around, "what do we know? We have an alleged unmarked cutting off a red, burgundy or brown van, depending on which version you listen to. The two, quote-unquote, cops jump out here," he said, moving away from the passenger side of the unmarked.

"The driver spreads out and covers the driver of the van about here," Natasha added, moving to the right of the body, three feet away.

"Then bam, bam, drop passenger," Rahjohn gestured like he was shooting at the body of the passenger lying under the white sheet.

"And bam, bam, male officer assailant drops driver unless you believe the lady from across the street. She says the female shot both victims. Wow, she's one tough chick," Natasha chuckled.

Rahjohn looked at the bodies under the blood stained sheets.

"Red van," he mused. "Remember the video tape from Jade East, the one with the burgundy MPV? Think it could be the same vehicle?"

"The same?" she echoed, considering the thought. "Possible...but not probable."

"Why not? I mean, what's the chance of two different murders in two different places, both involving reddish vans?" he challenged.

"That's assuming the van used here was red. We don't have positive ID yet, remember?" she reminded him.

Rahjohn began looking up and around, apparently at

the street.

"I wonder if there's any Red Light Surveillance camera's set up around here?" he thought out loud.

"Yeah, they're running through out the streets," she nodded. "I'll have it checked out."

Rahjohn kneeled down beside the driver's body and looked under the sheet. Then he moved to the passenger and did the same.

"What's up?" Natasha asked.

"I know these faces," Rahjohn answered, with the strain in his tone of a man frustrated by his own faulty memory. "I just can't place 'em."

"Too bad thugs don't carry ID's," Natasha cracked.

That's when the phone rang in Jay's pocket.

Rahjohn and Natasha looked at each other. The phone rang again as he reached in Jay's pocket. Pulling out the phone it rang a third a time and a fourth as he looked at the screen.

Restricted number.

He looked at Natasha. She shrugged. He answered it.

"Yo." Rahjohn answered the phone as if the call was definitely for him, still looking at Natasha to see if she was watching.

I don't know why I pay this man half the mind that I do.

Rahjohn could hear the mumbling of voices and then the sound of a young woman filtered through the line?

"What up, what's good?" she asked.

"It's all good, yo. What up, who dis?" Rahjohn asked in his best thug passion voice.

A brief pause, mumbled voices.

Click, the line went dead.

"She hung up," he said dumbfounded.

"I wonder why? Let me look at my notes. She? Umm...a girlfriend, maybe? And knows the man's voice and it ain't yours?" Natasha quickly replied, as he ignored her sarcasm.

"We'll never know," he sighed, "restricted number."

October 30, 2010
10:45 PM
Astoria, Queens

After setting the RX7 ablaze in an industrial section of Queens, Antoinette drove her purple Infinity G35 Coupe to the house she shared with Biz in Astoria. She had driven cautiously, keeping one hand protectively on the green book bag in the passenger seat. She didn't want to get stopped with a bag full of heroin, and the police were out in full force, not only because it was Mystery Night. It was also because of the two murder scenes she had helped orchestrate.

When Antoinette entered the house, Biz was pacing the floor, cell phone in hand.

"Hey, baby," Antoinette greeted him with a kiss. "You okay?"

"Yeah," he mumbled, resuming the pace.

"You sure, baby?"

Biz glanced at her, but didn't respond. He had just gotten word from the dude he sent to the Jade East that the police were all over the seedy motel.

"Did you see the MPV? The burgundy joint?" Biz asked.

"Naw, Dunn," his man replied.

Biz was perplexed with what had gone down at the motel. For starters, it was crawling with police. And the MPV wasn't there? Why? Did Jay get away? If so, why wasn't he answering his phone? And why was Bacardi so tense about the situation?

These were the thoughts that went through his mind, when he glanced at Antoinette, but all he mumbled was, "Some bullshit, yo."

Antoinette smirked to herself because she knew Biz didn't talk business with her, although she knew exactly what the problem was. Hell, she was the cause of it.

Antoinette moved towards him and wrapped her arms around his neck, then sucked his bottom lip.

"Well, if I can't help you solve the problem, maybe I can take your mind off of it for awhile," she grinned devilishly.

"Baby, not now. I got shit on my mind," Biz protested. But Antoinette was persistent.

"Then what better way to relieve the stress?" she cooed, then slowly lowered herself to her knees and began unbuckling Biz's jeans.

"Chill, ma," Biz protested weakly, but the growing bulge in his pants spoke louder than his words.

Antoinette stuck out her pierced tongue and circled the bell-shaped head of Biz's long and luscious dick. Applying pressure at the base then rotating her hand along the shaft, she stuck her tongue in the head of his dick then took the length of the dick into her mouth. Biz let out a guttural moan and his toes curled in his Tims.

Antoinette's head game had him fucked up. She was a true Captain and champion who handled her business. She ran her tongue down the length of his dick then sucked both his nuts. She then stuck it back in her mouth and began deep throating him harder. Biz grabbed a handful of her hair and began fucking her face with mounting intensity. When he came, it was with such force that it made him weak in the knees. He had to put his hand on her shoulders for support.

"Feel better?" Antoinette winked, getting up from the

floor and wiping her lips with the base of her palm.

The expression on his face said it all, but before he spoke his cell phone rang.

"Yo, ai-ight," he said then looked at Antoinette. "I'll be back."

"Bizzzz," she whined, "I thought we were going out."

"We are. I just need to handle something," he replied, fixing his pants then grabbing his keys and his coat.

"Okay," Antoinette replied, "just hurry up."

Biz winked then left. Antoinette pulled out her phone and hit Face.

"Yo, Nette, where you at? When you coming?" Face huffed, impatiently.

Antoinette peeked out the window to make sure Biz was gone then opened the door and headed for her car.

"I'm in Queens."

"Hurry yo' ass up, ma! We can't sit on this hot ass shit forever," Face remarked gruffly.

Antoinette looked both ways before opening her car door and grabbing the green book bag.

"I know, I know, baby. First thing in the mornin', I'll be over there," she said, taking the bag in the house.

"The mornin'?!" he thundered. "The fuck! You fucking crazy?! This MPVs on fire!"

"And I can't get away until then," Antoinette shot back then she softened her tone. "I promise baby, first thing. I gotta go."

She could hear him barking on her as she hung up. She looked around then decided on the closet. She took the book bag and put it behind a vacuum cleaner box. She smiled to herself. Everything was going perfectly. She knew Face would do what he had to do in order to keep the MPV safe. After all, the seven kilos of heroin she just put in the closet were supposed to be in the MPV hydraulic stash, only Face didn't know that but his greed would keep him from disappearing with the half a mill he was holding. A bird in the hand, but greed in the heart always keeps a man reaching.

October 30, 2010
11:22 PM
St. Luke's Hospital

"Nothing, Detective, nada. The guy wont even tell us his name," the officer told Rahjohn exasperatedly. "We're running his prints as we speak. Just waitin' on the results from the precinct, sir," the officer added.

Rahjohn sighed hard. Even though he wasn't officially assigned to the case any more, his gut was telling him there was something to this van involved.

"So what're we gonna do?" Natasha probed.

Rahjohn thought for a minute then smiled mischievously.

"When in Rome," he answered cryptically then turned to the officer. "How many officers in there?"

"One."

"Pull him out."

"Can't detective. Sorry, we were told…"

Remembering what Wilcox said, he cut the officer off. "Don't worry about it. I'll take the weight."

"Rahjohn, what are you about to do?" Natasha asked, sensing something in his smirk.

Rahjohn winked at her then turned to a passing doctor.

"Excuse me, doctor. Can I speak wit' you a minute?"

Dred lay in the hospital bed, eyes half closed and a slight smile on his lips. The pain killer the nurse gave him had him floating through the room. He couldn't even feel the gun shot he took in the thigh. The doctor had no problem pulling the bullet out, and now all Dred could think about was sleep, relaxing and going...

"You bitch ass nigga, scream and you're dead!"

Dred's eyes popped open real wide and he found himself staring down the barrel of a .45 automatic. The gunman was disguised in a doctor's coat and surgical mask, but the look in his eyes had him stuck.

"Man, I...," Dred stammered, looking around for the cop that had been in the room with him. He had never in his life wished to see a cop until that very moment. Where the hell are they when you need them?

The gunman put the gun to Dred's forehead and hissed, "What you tell the cops, nigga?"

"Nothin', yo, I swear."

"You thought we was gonna let you get away, huh?!"

"Come on man, I ain't got nothin' to do with that shit! That shit is between Baby Wise and Bacardi. He robbed Baby Wise, not me."

"Naw, muhfucka, it's between me and you! You fuckin' lyin'!"

"On my mother, son! I don't even fuck wit' Baby Wise like that! I was just there to hold Goo down! My word!" Dred pleaded.

The gunman slowly took the gun from Dred's head, and pulled the surgical mask from around his face to reveal Rahjohn's dazzling smile.

"Happy Halloween," Rahjohn winked then walked out.

Dred stared at Rahjohn's departing figure, confusedly. He didn't know if he had dreamed the whole thing or not. He was high; the only thing real to him was the feeling of warm piss coming down his leg out of fear.

Rahjohn came out holstering his unauthorized side arm.

"I got a name," he announced.

"How?" She asked, bemused.

His smirk said 'don't ask'.

"The name 'Bacardi' ring a bell?"

"Only with coke," she quipped.

Then come on, let me pour you a drink," he answered, heading for the elevator.

"Sean Murray, a.k.a. Bacardi was thirty-four years old and raised in Hollis," Rahjohn began as they drove.

"The name sounds familiar," Natasha remarked.

"Long juvey record, but squeaky clean since he turned legal."

"Smart or just lucky?"

"Both," he grudgingly admitted. "As well as extremely rich," he added. "Rumor has it that he made his first million by the time he was eighteen.

Natasha whistled, impressed.

"He's got his hand in a little of everything, but for the past five years, he's been trying to get legit," Rahjohn remarked bitterly.

Natasha looked at him.

"I detect more in your tone than a cop's dislike of criminals."

Rahjohn rode for a minute then answered.

"He's a fuckin' cop killer. A few years ago, a guy named Bennett, he was a good guy and a good friend. He just couldn't shake his past."

"How so?"

The car stopped at the light as Rahjohn looked out and off into the distance.

"A few dudes he grew up with in Brooklyn worked for

Bacardi. Bennett got mixed up in it and something, I don't know, something happened and Bacardi had him killed." Rahjohn explained then paused. "This fucking dude, man... he thinks he's the Black John Gotti or something. He's out here giving away turkeys and buying kids sneakers with one hand and destroying their parents and grandparents with the other."

Natasha didn't speak for a moment, allowing him to work his demons back in place then asked, "So what's his connection to this case?"

"That's the part I don't get," Rahjohn shook his head. "The Dred said Bacardi had robbed Baby Wise."

"Who's Baby Wise?"

"His government is Hakim Davis. But he goes by Baby Wise. Turns out him and his people are to Bacardi what Pappy Mason was to Fat Cat Nichols. If it's heroin in South Jamaica, then I guarantee it's got Baby Wise's stamp on it and Bacardi is his supplier," he explained.

"And Bacardi is supposed to be responsible for the Motel shooting? Maybe they had a falling out," Natasha proposed.

"But robbery? The type of money Bacardi is dealing with, whatever the deal was for wouldn't be worth the headaches."

"Ain't you heard? It's a recession, maybe even for heroin suppliers," she snickered.

"We're about to find out," Rahjohn replied.

He pulled over across from a busy strip club on Rockaway Boulevard. Cars were parked and double parked for half a block.

"Looks like your kind of place," Natasha remarked.

He ignored her feminine style signification.

"Just come on."

The brisk October night breeze swirled through the street, blowing trash tumbling across the street. Muffled bass notes thumped from several expensive whips, as fur and leather clad dons and divas made their way to the door. Not everyone made it inside though. In the time it took them to cross the street, Rahjohn saw at least four groups rebuffed by the two mountain-like bouncers.

The embarrassed couple or crews would slither away, watching with envy as others more fortunate were ushered in like ghetto royalty. When the bouncers saw Rahjohn and Natasha, their demeanor stiffened and they crossed their twenty two inch arms across their forty inch chests.

"Private party and ahh," bodyguard number one said, looking them up and down, "you don't look like the invited."

Three females in chinchilla, mink and sable snickered in Rahjohn's face as they disappeared inside.

Rahjohn held up his badge and Natasha then did the same.

"This enough bling for you?" Rahjohn remarked sarcastically.

Bodyguard number two's expression soured.

"This is a legal establishment and no law's being broken."

"Call it a surprise inspection then," Rahjohn smirked.

"That's the fire marshal's job," number two shot back.

"And the EMT's job is to pick up your Black ass after I beat it blue. Now get the fuck out of my way," Rahjohn hissed.

The eye boxing that ensued got so intense, that Natasha eased her hand closer to her holster. Bodyguard number one intervened seeing how ugly this could get for them.

"It's okay, Mac. I'm sure the officer has a valid reason for being here. Ain't that right, officer friendly?" He smirked menacingly.

"Open the door," Rahjohn demanded, in a no nonsense type tone. Reluctantly, the second bouncer complied. Once inside, Rahjohn and Natasha smelled the exotic blend of weed along with cigars and strong cologne. This was a gathering of Queen's elite. Diamonds glittered, platinum and gold twinkled and Guy Charlamagne by the dozens adorned table after table.

The emcee of the evening came out on stage wearing a pair of red Monkey jeans, a wife beater and a 40 inch platinum chain. In one hand was the mic, in the other a drink.

"Pimps up!" he bellowed into the mic.

"Hoes down!" several men in the audience shouted, rounding out the call and response.

"You goddamn right," the emcee chuckled. "Welcome to the freak of the week!"

The crowd clapped and hooted.

"Naw, Naw, I guess y'all ain't hear me. I said welcome to the freak of the week!"

The crowd got louder.

"That's what I'm talkin' about. Now to tell you regulars, ya'll know how it goes down e're week. But I see some new faces so I'ma run down the rules.

He stopped and took a sip of his drink.

"The competition is fierce and can be either man and woman, woman and woman, girl boys and boy girls, and any combination thereof except," the emcee emphasized, "man and man! So, if that's what you came to see, take yo' punk ass back to the Village."

The crowd laughed loudly.

"Other than that, the rules are ... ain't no rules! Be as freaky as you can and the winner gets five grand!" he announced holding up five fingers. "So let the games begin."

The crowd went wild as the three females from earlier, Chinchilla, Mink and Sable made their way to the stage. As they walked, they let their furs drop to the floor, revealing the fact that they were completely naked and only wearing stilettos. The shouts of approval shook the club. The deejay put on 50 Cents 'She Wants It' which drove the crowd into more of a frenzy.

Mink and Sable were both light-skinned with waist-like wasps and ass-like mules that jiggled like jello with every step. Chinchilla was honey brown and shaped like Beyonce. As soon as they reached the stage, Mink and Sable sandwiched Chinchilla, both kissing and licking down the length of her body, front and back.

"Goddam, they ain't bullshittin'!"

"Look at the ass on that bitch!"

The crowd salivated over the porn scene being done live right in front of their eyes. Mink, who was behind Chinchilla, stuck her tongue out then touched the tip of her own nose with it.

"Shit! That bitch got a tongue like a lizard!"

She spread Chinchilla's ass cheeks and began to slide her stiff tongue in and out her asshole, while Sable sucked Chinchilla's clit and finger fucked her four fingers to the knuckle. She gasped and cocked her leg up on Sable's shoulders, her pussy already milky and running down her thigh.

Rahjohn and Natasha watched, entranced by the spectacle. He had heard of freak of the week, but he had never seen if for himself. Now he had and the voyeur in him wouldn't let him turn away. Natasha finally cleared her throat after reluctantly tearing her own eyes away.

"What people will do for money, huh?"

"Yeah, I know," he responded, watching the three females get down on the floor. "He... ahh...he's probably up in V.I.P.," said Rahjohn still unable to tear his eyes away.

Above the ground level was a balcony with three booths overlooking the stage. Rahjohn looked up, scanning the booths for Bacardi, as he and Natasha headed up the stairs. He didn't see Bacardi, but

42

who he did see made him do a double take.

It was Autumn.

He would remember later, when it was much too late to turn back, that it was her eyes that grabbed him and wouldn't let go. The light hazel eyes that sparked with sensual attraction and made everyone and everything else fade into the background.

He flashed his badge at security and they admitted them into V.I.P. He kept his gaze on Autumn. Her eyes seemed to invite him and dare him to approach at the same time. But Rahjohn was more than up for the challenge, that is, until a familiar face stepped in the way, blocking her out and bringing him back to the reason for his presence.

"We got New York's finest in the house, ya'll", Bacardi smirked with eyes of stone. "What's up, detective? You and this pretty bitch come to compete for freak of the week?"

A smattering of laughter followed Bacardi's comment, but the atmosphere stayed tense. Natasha started to respond, but Rahjohn restrained her with a glance.

"Actually, naw Bacardi, we came to see if you had skipped town," Rahjohn remarked.

"Skipped town? Why would I do that? I'm the King of Queens!" he cracked, and a few 'yes' men nodded their agreement.

"You sure? That ain't what I'm hearin'," Rahjohn winked. He held up the mug shot of Jay and the other MPV victim. "You know these two?"

"Can't say that I do," Bacardi answered, taking a swig of his drink.

Despite Bacardi's poker face, Rahjohn could tell he had his attention.

"Oh, my bad," Rahjohn chuckled, pulling out a few more pictures and putting them on the table where Autumn and Bacardi were seated. He smiled but she didn't return it.

Bacardi glanced at the pictures and his heart

dropped. They were of Jay and the other dude dead at the murder scene.

Rahjohn sensed a tension in Bacardi's demeanor.

"Come on, Bacardi, it ain't a secret that Jay and Black worked for you. Evidently, somebody's declared war on you and you don't even know it," Rahjohn explained.

Bacardi's mind flashed back to Baby Wise's irate phone call. Of course Bacardi knew something had gone down at the Jade East, he just didn't know what, until now.

Bacardi looked up from the pictures, like, "worked for us? Doin' what? I never seen the dude before. And as far as war," he glanced around casually at the VIP area he was standing in as people were partying, drinking and having a good time all around him. "Does it look like I'm worried?"

Rahjohn nodded.

"Never seen him before, huh? That's your final answer?"

"Depends upon whether or not we should be having this conversation in the presence of my lawyer," Bacardi remarked snidely.

"Lawyer?" Rahjohn chuckled. "Naw, not at all. I just wanted to be the one to tell you your slip is showing," Rahjohn waited then looked at Autumn. "You should watch the company you keep, sweetheart, bystanders get it too."

"I'll take my chances," Autumn replied, with a hint of amusement in her tone.

"I could say the same thing about you", Bacardi sneered, turning to Natasha, "Don't end up like this clown's last partner."

Before Bacardi knew it, he was pinned against the bar and Rahjohn had Bacardi 40-inch Cuban link clutched in his had, choking Bacardi.

Biz and two others flinched like they were going for a gun. Natasha pulled out her gun and aimed it in their faces. "Please do!" she hissed. "So we can see whose mama gonna be praying for them tonight."

Meanwhile, Rahjohn was in Bacardi's' grill.

"You bitch made motherfucker, you don't wanna fuck with me! I promise you that!"

"You can't hide behind a badge forever nigga," Bacardi gritted. "Whenever you ready I'll be waiting!"

Rahjohn released him with a jerk.

"You better hope Baby Wise gets you first," Rahjohn growled, then turned away.

He went back to retrieve the pictures. Autumn was now standing like she was coming to Bacardi rescue and for some reason that irked Rahjohn.

"He ain't worth it, baby. Find another trick to juice," he spat, tucking the pictures back in his pocket.

"You're too fine to be a hater, papi," Autumn winked.

There eyes locked for a moment. Long enough for Rahjohn to realize Autumn was the most beautiful woman he'd ever seen, or at least, that's how he'd remember it. Maybe it was her energy of the moment because, right then, when he was admiring life's beauty, he was confronted with cold reality.

"Rahjohn, the door!" he heard Natasha bellow.

The urgency in her tone made him pull his gun. As he turned his attention to the first floor, several masked men were streaming into the room, then the sounds of "Oochie Wally" by Nas was drowned out by the chorus of automatic gunfire that filled the place.

Several patrons were instantly gunned down, including the two women and the man performing on stage. While half the hit team covered the main floor, the other half aimed for the V.I.P. section. As soon as Natasha warned him, Rahjohns instincts and training kicked in. He began firing on the shooters while simultaneously snatching Autumn by the arm and pushed her to the ground seconds before gunfire lit up the space that she had just vacated.

The Ace of Spades bottle shattered and wooden chips from the table burst into sawdust.

Not only were Rahjohn and Natasha shooting, so were a few of Bacardi's enforcers. Biz had fired a few shots then jetted to the emergency exit in the back of V.I.P. and disappeared.

Rahjohn aimed between the railings of the V.I.P. balcony and picked off two of the gunmen. He jumped through the air, dashing for cover behind the next booth to avoid a barrage of shots that sparked his previous position. Natasha had her aim on three more gunmen, all fell like wounded soldiers but the fourth tried to rush up the stairs into the V.I.P. room. Unfortunately, someone had the door locked. He blew a hole through the V.I.P. bouncer's head, causing him to lean and smash hard, tumbling down the stairs. The gunman's attention was on avoiding the bouncer's body as he fell past him, and when he looked up, Natasha fired twice hitting him in the neck and then the head, tearing away ski mask and flesh.

The last three gunmen backed out the entrance of the club and escaped. When the shooting finally stopped, and the metallic buzz of gunfire lingered, eleven people had been killed and six more injured.

Rahjohn turned his gun on Bacardi and his crew.

"Drop it! All of you!"

Reluctantly, they did.

"On your knees, hands behind your heads!" he ordered, approaching them, gun aimed.

"Come on, yo, you saw that shit. They was trying to kill us," one of the enforcers complained.

"Too bad they missed," Rahjohn hissed, locking eyes with Bacardi.

12:15 A.M.
Halloween

For the third time that night, Rahjohn found himself at another murder scene. The smell of death mixed with the lingering aroma of exotic blends of weed, as the crime scene investigators earned their pay checks. Chief Detective of Homicide Vernon Wilcox stepped through the carnage. His vision, focused like a scope, zeroed in on Rahjohn and Natasha.

"Griffin, what the hell is going on tonight?! You lettin' my Borough turn into the OK Corral on your watch?!" Wilcox scolded him. "I thought I told you I wanted this thing cleared up forthwith!"

"I'm trying, Sir," Rahjohn sighed, braced for the chewing out he knew he would get. "Unfortunately, every time I get somewhere on one body, somebody drops another."

"Don't get cute, John," Wilcox growled then turned to Natasha.

"And what about you? You think I promoted you for your looks?!"

"No Sir, I..." Natasha replied, but was cut off.

"You damn skippy, I didn't! I want results! Now what have you two got?" Wilcox demanded to know.

"From what we gather, it looks like a beef between Sean Murray and Hakim Davis," Natasha answered.

"Bacardi and Baby Wise?" Wilcox retorted, looking at Rahjohn, one eyebrow raised in surprise. Chief knew their government names as well as their street ones.

"I thought Davis was Murray's right hand man?"

"I guess there really is no honor amongst thieves, Vernon," Rahjohn remarked.

Wilcox sighed hard.

"If what you surmise is correct, we could have a blood bath on our hands."

"Not on my watch," Rahjohn winked.

"It better not be. The media is fucking having a reporter's wet dream, a big drug war with evidence of police involvement. Get this thing wrapped up, Griffin, you hear me?"

"Loud and clear," Rahjohn assured him.

Rahjohn and Natasha walked into the back office where Bacardi and Autumn were being held under the watchful eye of two uniformed officers.

"We got it from here, Stevens. Thanks," Rahjohn said.

"Sure detective. The other three guys, what are they being charged with?"

"They'll be charged with possession of a firearm; shooting in an occupied dwelling and hopefully murder if we can match ballistics," Rahjohn answered, never taking his eyes off Bacardi.

Bacardi returned the stare with seething hostility.

"What about these two?" the officer inquired.

Rahjohn knew all he had to do was say the word and he could railroad Bacardi into a murder rap. Bacardi knew it too. But Rahjohn didn't want to get Bacardi like that. He wanted to prove that he was smarter than Bacardi and beat him at his own game.

"Material witness, no charges," Rahjohn told him.

The officer left the room. Bacardi stood up.

"Where you think you going?" Rahjohn asked.

"You said no charges, right. Then I'm free to go," Bacardi replied.

"Sit down," Rahjohn told him.

"And if I don't?"

"Try me and find out."

Bacardi could see the look in Rahjohn's eyes and reluctantly sat down.

"Man, you wastin' your time. I ain't see shit and I don't know shit. I'm the victim here," Bacardi smirked.

"This ain't about what you know. It's about what I know," Rahjohn retorted. "See, I know you had Baby Wise's people set up at the Jade East. I know this because your people fucked up and left a witness. He says they were there to meet your people. So what's up, your money funny so you set up your main man? I've never known you to do bad business."

"Like I said yo, this is a waste of time," Bacardi said smugly as if Rahjohn didn't know jack.

"But see, you didn't want Baby Wise to know it was you, so you had your own people knocked off, so it wouldn't be obvious it was you. I mean, who is Jay and Black, peons; just pawns in the game, right?" Rahjohn taunted.

Bacardi chuckled, derisively.

"With an imagination like that, you should write a book."

"Oh, I am," Rahjohn smiled, like the wolf to the sheep. "And it's gonna be all about how I brought you down, because I'm this close," he said, holding his forefinger and thumb millimeters apart.

"Until then, can I go?" Bacardi asked, standing up and taking Autumn's hand in his own as she stood up too.

"How long you think your people gonna hold up under murder charges, huh B? A month, six months max and then they'll be singin' like canaries."

"Then you better keep them off the streets," Bacardi

replied, stone faced. He was through playing games.

Rahjohn nodded, sizing Bacardi up. Then he looked at Autumn. He could tell from earlier, she was Bacardi's weakness from the way he reacted when he spoke to her. So he decided to push again.

"Like I told you before Miss, he ain't worth it. They missed this time but what about the next time. Gimme a call if you ever need me... for anything," Rahjohn crooned, holding out his card to Autumn. His words were professional, but he made sure the flirtation was unmistakable.

Bacardi took the card from Rahjohn's hand, crumpled it up then dropped it on the floor.

"Like I told you... we don't know shit," Bacardi hissed.

As Bacardi escorted Autumn out, she fixed Rahjohn with a glance that Bacardi missed but Rahjohn didn't. In her eyes he saw fear, like she wanted to speak to him but she couldn't with Bacardi around. He knew he had to find a way to speak to her alone. Rahjohn wasn't the only one that caught the look. Natasha caught it too, along with the rhythm Rahjohn was throwing to Autumn and making no effort to hide it. When Rahjohn finally looked in her direction, she fixed him with a look of her own, rolled her eyes and walked away leaving him to watch the angry sway in her hips.

"Detective! Detective! Can you tell us what happened?

"Is this the beginning of a gang war?"

"Is it connected with the murders committed by the rogue detectives earlier tonight?"

The questions came in a barrage of words, one after the other, and as steady as automatic gunfire. Rahjohn and Natasha walked out of the club and into a sea of cameras.

The press was swarming around them like a group of frenzied sharks.

"There is no rogue detective," Rahjohn replied, pushing his way through the crowd of reporters.

"We're doing all we can to resolve this matter," Natasha added.

"Can you tell us more?"

"That's all we can say at this point."

"Is it that Sean Murray was the intended victim of the failed hit," a slim but buxom white woman asked, trailing behind them.

"Come on, Steph, gimme a break," Rahjohn said, opening his car door.

"Talk to me, Rahjohn. Don't I deserve special treatment?" she simpered flirtatiously. She was a reporter for the New York Daily News, and they knew each other well.

He stepped in the car, winked and replied, "When I know, you'll be the first to know."

"Liar," she giggled. "But I'ma hold you to it."

They pulled off.

"You fucked her, too?" Natasha asked with contempt.

"I don't do the white girls."

"Whatever," she hissed as she turned from him and looked out the car window.

"What's your problem, Tash?"

"Doesn't matter," she mumbled.

"It matters to me. You're my partner and I need to know that all that emotional... no, no, let me re-phrase that," he said choosing his words carefully, "I need to know that all this confusion isn't gonna take your focus," he said.

"My focus?!" she echoed with an exasperated chuckle. "What's that supposed to mean?"

"Just what I said," he said with a little attitude.

"Oh, so it wasn't my focus that yelled 'door'?! Huh?! Maybe if you had been focused on the right thing, I wouldn't

51

have had to warn your ass!" she huffed.

Irked by the truthfulness of her accusation, he lashed back. "Look, we ain't together, ai-ight?! I'm not tryin' to flip on you, I'm not tryin' to disrespect you, but we need a better understanding here. You and me are just f...," he caught himself before he finished and changed his words. "Friends... we're just friends."

"That ain't what you was about to say!"

"I said what I was about to say!"

"Be a man Rahjohn, goddamn it! I'm a big girl so say what you were going to say; we're just fucking, right?! That's what you were going to say, so there it is."

Rahjohn's temper was flared. He was ready to concentrate on the case and put an end to the nonsense. Natasha may've
been his partner professionally, but she needed to know her place in his personal world.

"This was a mistake," Natasha remarked. "It was a mistake to get involved with your trifling, immature ass. But it's cool because I can't blame nobody but myself. Unfortunately, some things you just can't take back," Natasha remarked, turning her face toward the window and winning the war against her tears. Rahjohn knew women well enough to recognize a certain hint of foreboding in her tone.

"What you mean, can't take back?" he probed.

"Just what I said," she retorted.

"Natasha," he said firmly.

"I'm pregnant, okay?!" she spat, turning to face him, eyes rimmed red and blazing. "I'm ....pregnant."

12:30 AM
HALLOWEEN

The bouncers never saw it coming....

In their mind, they didn't have anything to do with it. Baby Wise's people had contacted them out the blue and offered them twenty five hundred dollars a piece to leave the door at midnight, five thousand to just walk away? They jumped at the chance. They shouldn't have sold their lives so cheaply.

"Naw man, can't you hear? I said four whoppers, four large fries and six apple pies!" bouncer number two, who was also driving, barked into the drive thru speaker.

"Fuckin' Africans, man," bouncer number one chuckled.

The screech of the tires made them both turn their heads to the right simultaneously. Even if they would have had guns, it wouldn't have made a difference. The shooter was already jumping out of the back passenger seat of a blue '95 Lexus LS, a riot pump shotgun in his hands.

Boom! Click-Clack-Boom! Click-Clack-Boom!

The shooter worked the slide action quickly, releasing shots in rapid succession. He wasn't using buckshot. He was using solid body mangling slugs. The first broke the passenger window and burst bouncer number one's head like an exploding tomato.

"Nooo!" the driver yelled, shielding his face with his massive forearm and inner elbow, like his steroid-enhanced muscles could stop the destruction flying his way. One shot blew off his arm and the next opened his chest, the third took off half his face. The shooter aimed point blank at what was left of his target and burst it like a piñata with one final shot.

"Bitch ass niggas, that's from Bacardi," the shooter hissed, then jumped back in the car as it skidded off.

Three more shootings would occur through out the night. The temperature in Queens was rising as both squads turned up the heat on one another. The police were stretched thin and media provided blow-by-blow coverage, keeping the emphasis on the mystery detective involvement, of course.

Queens was on fire, so Bacardi and Baby Wise took to the mattress, Bacardi in Harlem and Baby Wise in Long Island.

Baby Wise's place in Wyandanch, Long Island was a simple sandy brick branch style home on Hickory Street. Baby Wise only used the place as a stash house and a retreat when the heat got heavy.

He and Vita entered the plush living room and turned on the lights, disengaged the alarm then tossed his coat on the small brown couch. The place was sparsely furnished and smelled stale because the door and windows were hardly ever opened. Vita had only been there a few times in order to drop off money for Baby Wise into the large safe installed in the floor of the master bedroom.

Baby Wise took a call, spoke briefly and gruffly then hung up.

"I can't believe this muhfucka!" Baby Wise grumbled more to himself than to Vita. "He fuckin' wit' the right one now though!"

Vita knew, despite Baby Wise's machismo, Bacardi's apparent betrayal had him confused. So she knew that she had to get in Baby Wise's head quicker, before he had a chance to think and figure out that everything isn't always what it seems.

"Baby, just like you taught me, trust no one," Vita reminded him, wrapping her arms around his waist. "His true colors is coming out because he fears you. He knows you're the one running South Side and you know how them Hollis niggas is. He's scared you too big to control."

Every word fed Baby Wise's ego and inflamed his sense of self.

"Indeed yo, indeed, this nigga ain't put in work like that anyway, not like me. Now he wanna go to war wit' a real soldier?!" he laughed and Vita laughed with him.

"He been feelin' himself baby, thinkin' his shit was sky blue. I mean... I didn't want to tell you but...." Her voice trailed off because she knew he'd pursue it.

"Tell me what?" he growled.

"I don't want to start nothin' but, he tried to holla at me at Club 2000 like a month ago." She lied but she was pouring it on thick to assure the success of the plan.

"What?" he based, grabbing her by the arm roughly. "Why the fuck you just tellin' me?"

"Because, I didn't want you to get mad. It wasn't nothing," she assured him trustfully because it never happened.

He slammed her against the wall.

"You wanted to fuck him, didn't you?!"

"No baby, I swear!"

"Didn't you?!" The rage at the thought of Bacardi touching Vita had him on fire and Vita knew how to play that fire even if it meant her ass.

"No baby," she answered, kissing him hungrily, "I don't want nobody but you."

"I'll kill you," he grunted between kisses, his hands feverously pulling up her skirt.

"I love you, baby...Wise," she cooed, snatching his belt loose and sliding her hands in his pants.

"I'ma kill that nigga," Baby Wise vowed, devouring Vita's tongue and hoisting her up on his waist.

Vita smiled to herself because she knew Baby Wise wouldn't turn back now. Even though the two teams had gone to war, no one of merit had died, and at the end of the day, it was about the money. Bacardi and Baby Wise were making a mint together, and either side could have called for a set down and squared the beef, but not now. Vita had made it personal.

"Humph, this my pussy, bitch, my pussy," Baby Wise grunted, bouncing Vita on his dick and hitting bottom with every stroke.

"Yes baby, your pussy, your pussy," Vita gasped, Baby Wise's snake slithering in and out of her womb. "Ohhh, fuck me, daddy!" She wrapped her legs around his waist and began grinding hard, taking him deep inside her.

"Damn this pussy is fuckin' good," Baby Wise moaned, sweat beginning to bead up on his forehead.

"It's yours daddy, all yours," Vita groaned. "Oh...oh b...baby, I'm about to...."

That's all she got out before her whole body tingled and exploded all over Baby Wise's dick. The way she squealed when she came always sent Baby Wise over the edge. He came right behind her, pressing his body violently against hers.

"Goddamn I love you, girl," he crooned, kissing her face. Vita laid her head on his shoulder, feeling the moment. The plan was coming off, almost too easy. She was glad they had thought of it.

1:00 AM
HALLOWEEN

Bacardi pulled his platinum Aston Martin Vanquish into the parking lot of McDonald's in Harlem about the same time Biz pulled in from the opposite direction in a black Porsche Cayenne. They got out, leaving Autumn and Antoinette in their respective cars. The two females nodded casually then Autumn turned back to watching the Wire on her iPhone.

Bacardi and Biz moved close to the end of Biz's Porsche.

"Yo fam, what the fuck is goin' on?!" Bacardi seethed, pacing a few feet then back, his words coming out in the puffs of smoke of the early morning air.

"This is crazy, Dunn. Them niggas ran up in that place and murdered everything movin'," Biz emphasized, bouncing on the balls of his feet to keep warm.

"You heard about Jay and Black?"

"I'm still on it. We'll know..."

"We already do, them niggas is dead."

"Dead?" Biz echoed

Bacardi nodded, watching Biz closely and scrutinizing his reaction.

"That's what the fuckin' cop came to show me, Jay and Black wit' they wigs pushed back, yo."

"Get the fuck outta here," Biz replied then thought for a minute and added, "So, somebody hit Baby Wise people and us, on the same night?!"

"Yeah, but Baby Wise thinks that somebody is us," Bacardi sighed with frustration. The last thing he wanted was beef. Beefs cost money and were counterproductive. But now that Baby Wise had tried to kill him, there was no turning back.

"You take care of the bouncers?" Bacardi asked.

"Done, banged 'em up. They hollered back at our gambling joint on 205th, but it wasn't about shit. Fuck 'em, they in over they head," Biz bragged.

"Still in all, we got more to lose, especially wit' this fuckin' cop Griffin on my dick. This nigga been wantin' to get at me ever since that Brooklyn thing," referring to the incident from long ago wherein one of Rahjohn's closest friends were killed. "So we gonna cook this beef slow, aight?"

"I hear you Dunn, but you know how Baby Wise do, Dunn goes hard."

"Indeed so, but let me worry about that," Bacardi instructed. "You worry about finding the niggas that killed Jay and Black 'cause that's the root and the rest of this shit is branches."

"No doubt B, I got you," Biz assured him.

They shook hands with a gangsta hug then got back in their cars. Bacardi didn't pull right off. Instead, he watched Biz leave, watching his brake light illuminate then disappear before he left the parking lot.

"What's up baby?" Autumn asked.

Bacardi, still looking in the rear view mirror, answered cryptically, "Who benefits from this?"

"Benefits from what?" she questioned, still watching

the Wire.

Instead of answering her question, he answered with another.

"You know how to catch a snake, baby?"

"How?"

He looked at her and smirked.

"With a rat...a hood rat. We get at the nigga's broad, Antoinette. See, if you can't catch me a snake."

Autumn nodded her understanding.

1:15 AM
HALLOWEEN

Face and Mellow headed back to East New York in Mellow's navy blue Dodge Charger. They had taken the MPV to Mellow's grandmother's house in Bed Sty. She had a garage, and after clearing it out, they stashed the MPV in it. They pulled up to Tank's apartment building off of New Lots Avenue and parked the car behind Face's '02 BMW 745i. When Face stepped out of the car, he heard the rumble of music coming from above. He looked up and could tell the music was coming from Tank's apartment. A few shadows moved past the window which gave the impression that the place was packed.

"What the fuck is that nigga doin'?" Mellow gritted.

"Stupid muhfucka," Face mumbled as they entered the building. When they got to the third floor and approached Tank's door, the music was seeping under the door and through the cracks.

Face pounded on the door until Bop hollered, "Who?"

"Nigga, open the fuckin' door," Face barked.

When he did, Face pushed past him and into the living room. He saw four chicks dancing in thongs and stilettos, scattered bills at their feet. One brown skin Dominican chick gave Tank a lap dance while he smoked a blunt of wet or dust as the formaldehyde was called in the hood. The sharp, pungent odor filled the room and turned

Face's stomach. He snatched the stereo plug out of the wall so hard, sparks flew from it.

The chicks turned to look at him.

"Get the fuck outta here," he said calmly but firmly. The Dominican chick got off Tank's lap and approached Face seductively.

"Como esta, papi, don't act like..."

That's all she got out before Face yoked her by the throat and moved her toward the door. The force made her hit the ground, but her anger made her get back up, spitting a razor into her hand in one smooth motion. She came at Face her razor poised to strike and found herself with a .45 caliber automatic to her head.

"Now what?" Face remarked calmly.

She backed away, lowering the razor, her eyes promising him a different outcome next time.

The other four chicks grabbed their coat and their clothes and headed for the door. Mellow locked it behind them as Face turned to Tank.

"Yo, son, what the fuck is you in to? Up in here smokin' dust wit' the music blastin' and shit. Yo, you slippin', son, word," Face spat, tucking his pistol.

Bop sat down next to Tank and took the blunt. Tank blew out smoke from his mouth and nostrils and smiled.

"Please, nigga, never that I'm the fuckin' Matrix, son, explode in this bitch into a bunch of zeroes and ones."

Face chuckled, shaking his head as he perched himself on the arm of the loveseat. "Nigga, that's that dust talking shit."

"Yo, when is this bitch 'posed to get here?" Bop asked lazily, inhaling the embalming smoke.

"In the mornin'," Face replied, lighting a cigarette.

"Man, fuck that," Tank spat, talking with his hands the way he did when he was dusted. "Let's just take the MPV to them Spanish niggas on Atlantic. I know they can find that shit up in there."

"You sound stupid, B. That whip been all over the news. The wrong muhfucka see that car and the fuckin' police be all over us. Shit's a fucking wrap," Face retorted.

"True, true," Tank nodded, in between tokes on the blunt. "Besides....we need that bitch here, so we can burn her and the truck."

Bop and Mellow nodded their agreement.

"Whoa yo, fuck you talkin' about? We aint burning shorty. Shorty good," Face protested.

Tank leaned forward, putting his elbow on his knees.

"Naw son, that shit is non-negotiable. Shorty gotta go."

"Word Face, Tank is right. You said it yourself, everybody had to die, but we fucked up now. It's a loose end runnin' around. You think shorty gonna hold water if the heat come down?" Mellow explained, slouched on the couch.

"Fuck no she not," Tank answered for him.

Face looked at his three cohorts. He may've been the de facto leader, but none of them were yes men. And what they said made sense. The problem was Face was smart enough to adapt to any situation. Shorty was a real ride or die chick and she had that snapper. Face wanted to protest, but he could tell he was outvoted.

"What a waste," he grumbled, blowing out smoke.

1:15 AM
HALLOWEEN

Rahjohn and Natasha drove to the precinct in a tense silence, both alone in their thoughts. Natasha was upset with herself for even telling Rahjohn. What did she think his reaction would be? He had already made it clear that he wasn't ready for a committed relationship. What made her think he was ready for a child or another child for that matter? She didn't even know if he already had kids. She cursed herself for her momentary weakness, thinking maybe, the fact that she was carrying his child would change something, that it would hit him like an epiphany and he would see a new light, a more complete light.

Yeah right, she thought bitterly, balling the idea up in her mind like a piece of paper and trashing it in the bin of wishful thinking.

Rahjohn was vexed, shaking his head subtly from time to time at his own thoughts. He was full enough of himself to think maybe Natasha had gotten pregnant on purpose in order to trap him, like pregnancy depended on a woman's will and not on the biological act. Then again, she might not even be pregnant. That was his next thought. How many times had he heard that before from a woman beginning to feel his neglect or trying to play him out of a few hundred for a supposed abortion?

But deep down he knew Natasha wasn't a hood rat or a gold digger, and as he remembered the look in her eyes when she told him, he knew she was serious.

He pulled up into the precinct parking lot, sighed and turned to Natasha.

"Look, Tash, I..."

That's as far as he got before Natasha got out of the car and slammed the door in his face.

"Okay," he said to himself as he got out of the car.

When he entered the squad room, Natasha was pulling out the chair to her desk, which was against his so they faced each other when they sat down. Before Rahjohn sat down, detective Joseph Little approached.

"Hey, the tape from the traffic got here fifteen minutes ago. Where you been?"

"That was quick. I wasn't expecting it for another week," Rahjohn remarked sarcastically as he and Natasha followed Detective Little to the computer monitor.

"You can thank Wilcox. Word is he personally put a foot up Transit's ass, he gave 'em shoe leather for tongues," Little chuckled. "So, they asap'ed it on the double."

Natasha and Rahjohn leaned over both of Little's shoulders as he punched up the video sequences. As the video of an intersection on Linden Boulevard came up, Little commented, "These cameras are convenient, but they're a pain in the ass, too. I'm glad my wife doesn't have access to shit like this. She'd never speak to her sister, again," Little snickered.

"Here we go," Rahjohn said, seeing the MPV pull up to the light. "Can you zoom in?"

"Sure thing," Little answered, and punched it in.

The camera was close enough to see Jay and Black's faces and the license number. Natasha wrote down the plate.

"Natasha, write down that plate," Rahjohn said not paying attention to the fact that she already was.

"Already on it."

"Run it. We might get lucky, you never know."

The MPV made a left as they continued to watch the screen two cars back, they saw Vita and Bop in the Crown Victoria.

"Bingo! We got our perps," Rahjohn said excitedly over his shoulder to Natasha.

She came back over.

"Run it back," Rahjohn told Little.

The frame it froze on gave him a partial view of Vita's profile. It was grainy and concealed by the night, but it was enough for Rahjohn to get a visual in his head.

"Want me to run it back to get that license plate too?" Rahjohn shrugged.

"You can, but I guarantee it's stolen and probably a burnt out shell by now."

"Yeah, you're probably right."

Natasha came back over from her computer and handed him a printout. Rahjohn looked at it and nodded.

"Now it's beginning to make sense," Natasha remarked.

"You must be reading my mind," Rahjohn winked.

"That it's either one of two things. One, Renee Owens was the inside man on the job, but got exed out of the equation," Natasha surmised.

"Or somebody else set it up, but they had to kill Renee because she knew 'the somebody's' face," Rahjohn added.

Little took the printout from Rahjohn.

"Who's this?" he asked.

"One of the victims from the Jade East murders, she was the night manager," Natasha explained then looked at Rahjohn. "Either way, this probably takes Bacardi out of the picture. He really is the victim."

"Yeah, so who benefits?" Rahjohn asked taking the same angle as Bacardi took.

The phone rang and Little answered.

"That's what we get paid the big bucks to find out," Natasha joked.

"Yeah, right, they get any bigger and I might even be able to afford a whole apartment," Rahjohn quipped.

Little hung up and looked at them.

"Found a burnt up yellow Mazda RX7 still smokin', over near Belt Parkway."

"No surprise there. Let us know if the old hooptie Buick turns up. Check Manhattan and King's County," Rahjohn told him, as he and Natasha turned to leave.

"So what's the next move?" she asked.

"Let's go by Renee's place and see what we can find."

Natasha nodded.

"Hey," Little called to them, the phone receiver between his ear and shoulder as they both turned together looking back at him. "Anybody ever tell you, you two make a helluva team?"

1:33 AM
HALLOWEEN

Grip pulled his money green Mercedes out of a parking spot and headed down the street toward the light.

He had been picking up money from several spots Baby Wise had in Baisely Park Houses. He popped in Fifty's 'Get Rich or Die Tryin' CD just as a pick-up truck in front of him stopped abruptly causing him to suddenly halt. In turn, this caused an Escalade to ram him from behind. He automatically recognized a set up, as two dudes popped up from the bed of the pick-up and leveled their AR-15 scopes at his head. Grip laughed in their faces.

"Go head, muhfuckas, shoot!" He taunted them because his windows were all bulletproof.

Someone tapped on his window with something metallic. He assumed it was a gun at first. But when he turned and looked, his eyes got big. In a gloved hand, the man at his window smiled brightly as he held a grenade between his thumb and pointer finger. In his other hand, a piece of tape, which he used to tape the grenade to the window then he leaned down so Grip could see his face.

"We already know your shit is bulletproof, nigga. But this here is a little bit bigger than a bullet," the dude said, smiling as he tapped the grenade. So, now we can see if your shit is grenade-proof nigga, ya heard?"

"Nigga, fuck you," Grip barked, but his upper lip was quivering.

The dude shrugged. "Okay," then reached to pull the pin as he hollered across the street to his mans and 'em. "Get ready to fall back, ya'll!"

"Yo chill, Dunn," Grip relented.

"Huh?" the dude taunted.

"Chill! I'ma toss the money out, just take that shit off my window."

The dude laughed at him.

"Yo, yous a funny nigga. Yo, son, this ain't no robbery. Somebody wanna talk to you."

The dude pulled out a cheap flip, pressed send twice then put the phone to his ear.

"He right here."

The dude held the phone up to the window.

Grip looked at him skeptically.

"Duke, you good," the dude assured him, then peeled the grenade from the window.

Grip lowered the window just enough to take the phone then put it back up.

"Who th..."

"You recognize the voice?"

"Huh?"

"My voice, I said you recognize?"

"Yeah, yeah," Grip said knowing better than to speak the man's name. He quickly added, "Yo man, I ain't have nothing..."

Bacardi cut him off, calmly.

"Sure you did, you had everything to do with it, but I don't blame you 'cause you ain't the boss. Bosses give orders, not take 'em. You ever think about that?"

"Think about wh..."

"Being a boss?"

"What you mean?" Grip asked, not seeing the relevance in the question.

"I'm sayin', the ship is going down but you ain't gotta go down with it. You know that nigga tried to get me killed tonight?"

"Who?"

"You know goddamn well who, Grip. Don't play dumb with me. I hate dumb people. I only do business with smart people. You wanna do business with me, Grip?" Bacardi offered. Grip was beginning to catch on.

"What kind of business?"

"Your man can't go to war wit' me, my money too long," Bacardi laughed. "I fuckin' made that nigga and this is how he repays me? Fuck it, I ain't mad. I made him. I can make another one and this time I'll name him Grip. Do you understand?"

Grip understood perfectly.

"Yo son, I'm sayin', Baby Wise is my..."

Bacardi cut him off.

"No names, Dunn, but you understand, right?" Bacardi repeated.

"Nah, but I can't..."

"Think, nigga! This is chess, not checkers yo, stay seven moves ahead. If the shoe was on the other foot, he'd been done jumped the fence and slit your throat. Ain't no more loyalty in this game, and you know it. Now what up, yes or no? They die, you live or you die with them.

Grip didn't take long to think it over.

"I'm saying, what I gotta do?" he asked with a sheepish eye of anticipation.

He could hear Bacardi smiling through the phone.

"I knew you were a smart man. Now where's this nigga's mattress at?"

2:00 A.M.
HALLOWEEN

Rahjohn and Natasha had gone to Renee's building on 226th Street, near Merrick Boulevard. Outside, the building was nothing to brag about, but inside, the place was laced with expensive accruements.

"Yeah, the girl was definitely on the payroll," Rahjohn remarked, running his hand along the 55" inch plasma TV.

"Yeah, but whose?" Natasha quipped.

Rahjohn sat down in the black leather massage chair and clicked it on.

"Mmmm, this is what I'm talkin' 'bout, baby. Oh yeah, this feels great," he said his eyes closed as he began to relax for a moment. "I'm guessing she was on Bacardi's payroll."

"What makes you say that?"

"This is Hollis, Bacardi's stomping grounds. He probably used the motel to handle transactions. There's probably a few kilos stashed there, some money too." His voice trailed off for a moment. "I gotta get me one of these. You wanna try it?" he said finally opening his eyes.

Natasha shook her head.

"Remember when you asked who benefits?"

"Yeah?" he answered.

"Neither Bacardi or Baby Wise, think about it. This ain't a beef, it's a robbery."

Rahjohn thought then replied, "Looks that way, and Renee seems to be the link between both cases."

"Exactly, she was in a perfect position to know how everything was going down. She gets together a little team and makes it happen only the team had other plans for her. She sets up Bacardi and they set her up."

"Nothing beats the cross, but the double cross," Rahjohn quipped then added, "And I'll tell you something else. There's something real valuable in that MPV. It has to be, they went through too much to get it," Rahjohn declared.

"If that's the case, if Renee did set the whole thing up then we need to run her phone records. Chances are we'll find a number or two to hang our hat on. Hopefully, they weren't smart enough to use a prepaid," Natasha suggested.

"Yeah, 'cause then we'd be back to square one, which is back to nothing and Wilcox definitely ain't tryin' to hear that," Rahjohn said.

"So, we jump on it first thing in the morning"

"No doubt."

"Rahjohn snuzzled in the chair and turned it up a level.

"Aaahh," his voice trailed off.

"Umm, Rahjohn."

"Hmmm."

"We have to go."

He cracked one eye and smirked.

"Can I take the chair?"

"I can't," said Natasha shaking her head as she turned from him and walked away.

By the time they reached Natasha's brownstone in Bed Sty, they had lapsed back into an uncomfortable silence. As long as it was work-related, their rhythm was smooth and easy. But as soon as they were on personal time, the rhythm became warped, like a record under the heat of the sun.

"Tash, we really need to talk about this."

"So talk."

"I mean, I'm just saying," Rahjohn struggled to find the words, so he settled for something simple. "What are we gonna do?"

Inside, Natasha warmed to the fact that he said the word 'we' and not 'you' like it was her problem.

"Well, right now, I'ma take a shower then crash. I'm exhausted."

Rahjohn nodded, then casually replied, "So you're sleeping alone?"

Natasha glanced at him then shook her head with a slight smirk. As she got out the car, Rahjohn got out right behind her, his eyes glued to her ass. He loved her walk, toes pointed out like a ballerina, head held up and the soft, sensual sway in her hips. He thought about how she'd put on heels and he'd tell her to walk nasty. Her strut alone made him rock hard. He hoped that the fun they shared wasn't about to end, now that she had a baby on board.

When they entered her apartment, Natasha said over her shoulder, "Since I'm buying, you can at least play bartender," then disappeared upstairs.

When she came back, she had her hair in a ponytail and was wearing a pair of oversized sweat pants and Washington Redskins jersey. Rahjohn handed her a drink he had poured. They both settled on the couch, a friendly distance between them, Natasha put her bare feet on the coffee table, crossed at the ankles and clicked on the TV.

"Ahhhh, this feels good" she cooed. "I'm starving but I'm too tired to eat."

"I told you, you would be," Rahjohn reminded her with a chuckle.

She giggled.

"Oh, believe me, I was gonna eat your shit up, but,"

she shrugged, "duty called."

"Yeah, you know why they call us one-time?"

"No why?"

"Because they can get away a thousand times, but all we need is one time," he explained.

"Makes sense?" she agreed to their little inside humor. "Better than 5-0," she snickered.

"What made you want to be a police officer?" Rahjohn smiled.

She looked at him, her expression indignant.

"You really want to know?"

He nodded as she pulled her feet under her and rested her head in the palm of her hands, her elbows resting on the back of the couch.

"I did it for my father. He was a bank robber," she told him, watching his reaction.

"Okay," he responded, in a tone that said I'm listening.

"I mean, he wasn't like a bad person or just a stone cold killer, but D.C. in those days was crazy. Seems like everybody's father or uncle robbed banks. I grew up with a pack of kin like that. To us it was just normal, I guess" she explained, then took a deep breath. "Anyway, my father was my world. He took care of his family, made sure we never wanted for anything. Then one day, he didn't come home."

Her eyes stayed dry, but Rahjohn could tell it was only because she had already cried her whole life over it. Still, he could hear the tears in her voice.

"We lived in the projects, you know, Barry Farms, so of course nobody knew anything, nobody seen anything, you know how it is, don't talk to the police and all that stuff," she shook her head. "And in a way, I can understand that, but what kills me is nobody did anything, either!" She paused for a moment. "I mean it ain't like nobody knew my daddy. He was always helping somebody, but when he was bleeding to death in that parking lot, nobody remembered that," she remarked bitterly. Rahjohn moved over closer and put his arm around her. She leaned forward, elbows on knees, away from his embrace.

"I'm okay," Natasha assured him then went on with her story. "My mama has family in Flushing, so we moved. It was my mom, me and my brother; I was thirteen. But I never forgot what happened and the sight of my father dying in the street. I promised my daddy the last time I saw him at his funeral that I'd get whoever was responsible."

"So you became a cop so you could track down your father's killer?"

Natasha nodded.

"But along the way, I found a lot of little girls and boys whose daddy wasn't coming home and it made me realize the world is bigger than just my problem, you know?"

Rahjohn moved forward and replied, "Yeah, I know exactly what you mean. Tell me something, do you still feel the same way? If you saw the guy now, and knew it was him, would you still take revenge? What would you do?" he asked.

She looked at him as the thought went through her.

"I'd blow his head off with a smile on my face."

Rahjohn nodded in understanding. He wasn't the type of cop who thought his badge was a license to kill. But he was tough. He prided himself on being fair and although what Natasha was saying was in essence a crime, he truly couldn't blame her.

She bumped her body against his, playfully.

"You remind me of my father," she smirked then ran her hand over his waves. "Same smooth complexion, your wit and you have the type of smile that can make a girl wanna believe every word you say," she smiled.

Rahjohn deep down was comfortable with Natasha and comfortable with her having his child. Actually, he wanted her to have the baby. He planned on doing all he

could to be a good father. He would be the best father that
there ever was. And a part of him wanted to be the man that
he knew she needed him to be. And as much as he wanted to
do right by her, he knew deep down he wasn't quite ready.
Still, he would stand by her side one hundred percent and be
there for her and their child. Rahjohn wanted to say
something to convey his feelings. He just didn't know the
words.

"Listen Tash, this thing..."

She softly touched his finger to his lips.

"Don't, please, I heard you loud and clear earlier.
Besides, I already knew you were no good for me. But like a
moth to a flame I couldn't help myself," she said, as she
leaned closer to him. "I wish I had the power to let you go,
but I can't get you out my system," she said aloud, as she
quenched her sensual thirst with a taste of his lips.

Rahjohn pulled her on top of his lap as Natasha
willingly straddled him. Each kiss they shared became more
and more intense as passion heated between them. Rahjohn
abruptly pulled his tongue from her mouth so he could pull
her football jersey over her head, revealing a firm pair of
perfect C cup breasts that Rahjohn loved nothing more than
to suck on. Natasha momentarily fumbled with Rahjohn's
belt until she got it loose then unbuckled his pants and
dropped them around his ankles as she slid to her knees.

"Mmmm," Rahjohn moaned, as Natasha gripped his
long, curved dick. She ran her tongue around the head
before wrapping her lips around the shaft, then proceeding
to devour his manhood greedily.

Rahjohn had to exert every ounce of restraint not to
cum in her mouth, because he wanted to fuck her. He pulled
her off her knees, urging her to ride him.

"You want this pussy, baby," she cooed wistfully,
sliding out of her sweatpants and straddling him.

"Hell yeah," he grunted, gripping his dick and

positioning it to slip it inside her.

Natasha gripped the back of the couch as Rahjohn penetrated her wetness, grabbing her hips and forcing her to take every inch.

"Oh yeah, oooh fuck this pussy, baby," she urged him, digging her nails in the couch.

Natasha repositioned herself, putting her feet on the couch and squatting on Rahjohn's dick. Then she held his hand, leaned back and began grinding his dick.

"You like it like that, baby? she huffed lustfully. Cum in this pussy, baby, cum with me."

"You love this dick, don't you?"

"Yes!"

"Huh?!"

"Yes daddy, I lo..., I'm, I'm..." Natasha gasped, leaning forward and wrapping her arms around his head and burying his face in her juicy titties.

Rahjohn grabbed her ass and pounded her pussy relentlessly, making her cum hard and himself even harder. Sweaty and spent, she rested her head against him knowing all to well, he had her open and there was nothing she could do about it.

2:00 A.M.
HALLOWEEN

The penthouse suite was packed to capacity. It was a cavernous room with cathedral high ceilings that led out to a patio, complete with a pool that overlooked Manhattan. It had once belonged to the Rockefellers, but recently had been bought by the host of this party, hip hop music mogul: Jay Malone. Better called by his single initial, J was known for doing things big, so of course his Halloween bash couldn't just be on Halloween. It had to be a Halloween weekend, including Mystery Night, when the party would begin and not end until the first of November, All Saints Day. He spent hundreds of thousands of dollars to have the best Hollywood theatrics and atmosphere. And even though he spent a small fortune, there was a method to his madness. He had sold the rights to M.T.V., convincing them to air his Halloween Weekend Bash. He walked away from the table making a couple of million.

Celebrities of all kinds from the music, sports and television industry walked around in costumes that ranged from quite simple to quite scandalous. Dwight Howard came dressed in his trademark Superman suit, while Megan Goode came as a belly dancer attached to some model type

Latino dressed as a bull fighter. A few females wore nothing but fluorescent colored body paint and stilettos. The only one not outfitted in Halloween splendor were the street dudes in attendance, not too many, but enough for J. Malone to keep his street credibility reputation. That was how Kane ended up at the party. J. Malone, born and raised in Jamaica, Queens idolized dudes like Baby Wise and Kane. They were in the same bloodline as cats like Ronnie Bumps, Fat Cat Nichols and the Supreme Team niggas and these were the cats J. Malone wanted to be mentioned with. So, when he spotted Kane and his three man entourage, he walked right over.

"Kane, my nigga! What's poppin' yo?!" J. Malone, dressed as a Roman emperor, greeted Kane with a handshake and a hug.

Kane chuckled, looking him up and down. "Who you 'posed to be in a fuckin' skirt and sandals?"

"Nigga, this ain't no skirt, it's a toga! I'm Caesar, the first President of the United States!" he joked. But his comment went right over Kane's head. J waved it off and added, "It's for the cameras, yo. All them white bitches out there is wonderin' what's under a niggas' toga, ya heard!"

Kane and the crew laughed.

"I dig it, my dude. Do your thing," Kane chuckled.

J. Malone, conspiratorially and without a smile added, "I heard about that shit earlier. I know that's why Baby Wise ain't come. He good?"

Kane wasn't surprised word had already reached J, but he wasn't about to discuss it with him, so he fudged.

"Yeah, man, niggas blow shit outta proportion. Shit wasn't serious, yo, Baby Wise good."

J Nodded.

"You sure? 'Cause you know, I got peoples, yo... All I gotta do is say the word."

The smile in Kane's eyes threatened to explode to

78

laughter at the music mogul, wanna be gangster in front of him.

"Naw, we good, yo. I appreciate that."

"No doubt you my dude yo. I fuck wit' you."

"Indeed."

"I'ma circulate. But, if you need me, just holla," J. Malone told him, giving him a departing hug.

"Yeah J, we'll call you," Kane smirked, then after J, Malone walked away, he turned to his crew. "You hear this bitch ass nigger? He got peoples."

They laughed at J. Malone as he walked away greeting guest after guest as if he was really that nigga.

"This clown ass nigga really letting this shit go to his head," one of Kane's lackeys remarked.

"Like he said, its all for the cameras," Kane cracked.

What he didn't know was, very shortly it would be him and his crew that the camera were focusing on.

Baby Wise trusted no one with his whereabouts of his get away spot. So once Grip made the decision to join Bacardi's team, he couldn't tell them about Baby Wise but he could tell them about Kane. He knew exactly where Kane was, because after he did the rounds, that's where he was headed. He even gave his pass to get in to the dude who had taped the grenade to his window who was currently getting off the elevator and entering the penthouse dressed as the black Lone Ranger.

He hadn't had much trouble getting in, even though he had two guns in his black plastic gun belt. Security on the ground floor had looked at them skeptically for a moment until he pulled the one in his left holster out, twirled it around his finger and pulled the trigger. The toy cap went off with a plastic bang like a fire cracker. He winked at the security guard who chuckled. Then two females dressed in scantly Indian costumes approached taking security's attention, and the Lone Ranger was waved on.

As he got off the elevator, he looked around. At first glance, he could see at least six other cowboys and it made him smile, because he would blend right in with his black mask and fake, thick, moustache with the pirate curls on both ends. A Coco look-a-like sashayed by dressed in a Wonder Woman costume and he watched her ass jiggling all the way. *A white woman with a fat ass, what is the world coming to?*

He scanned the crowd until he spotted Kane standing with some dude dressed in a Roman outfit and two chicks naked except for body paint and he made his way through the thick crowd. His gun in his left holster may've been fake, but the .38 long nose in the right holster and the .44 bulldog in the small of his back were as real as they come. All of a sudden he felt a gun in his back.

"Don't move!" the voice boomed and he froze until he heard the man breakup in laughter.

He whirled around to find a drunken white dude that was obviously gay, wearing a cowboy outfit and holding a fake gun.

"Wow, cowboy, I like your gun," the white dude said impishly.

In any other circumstance, he would have broke the faggots jaw, but he was on a mission so he hissed, "You're a lucky muthafucka..."

He quickly turned around to Kane and continued to approach him through the moving crowd. As he got to where he wanted he wanted to be, he pulled out the .38 and cocked it.

"Yo, Kane," he yelled.

Kane turned in the direction of the voice, but had no time to react as the dude raised the .38 and put two in his head and one in his heart in rapid succession. Even with the music blaring, the gunshots rang out in unmistakable clarity. The place broke out in pandemonium and bodies began running, pushing and shoving in a mad rush to get to the exit.

What the hit man wasn't counting on was Kane's people being strapped. But, J. Malone wanting to be down, escorted them in personally, so they weren't searched by security. For this reason, as soon as the first two shots entered Kane's head, his three man team less than three feet away, drew down and opened up. The gunshots rang out, two hitting the hit man, one in the shoulder the other in his side. Quickly, he grabbed the first body he could to use it as a human shield. And who did he grab; it was none other than J. Malone. With all his strength, he swung J. Malone around in front of him to absorb the oncoming man slaughter. J Malone's world went into slow motion as the irony of the moment played out in his mind. And it was, that the same gun's he helped get in were the gun's riddling his body, taking his life and J had a good life.

The hit man thought he was protected until he felt the piercing and immediate burning sensation in his stomach. One of the shots went straight through J and exploded in his stomach.

He staggered back, firing and managing to drop one of the three dudes that would later die. He looked down at the blood spurting from his stomach and took aim once more. But, it was to no avail. The dead body of J. Malone fell to the floor leaving the hit man exposed to the ballistic onslaught of Kane's two remaining men. He was hit so many times he was dead before he hit the floor.

The two remainders then merged with the frenzied crowd grabbing a mask here, a hat there, until they were disguised enough to slip right through the net of the N.Y.P.D.

2:39 A.M.
HALLOWEEN

"Witnesses say that the gunshots erupted in the middle of the room, in J. Malone's immediate vicinity. The gunman, some say dressed as a cowboy, others say, dressed as a policeman, killed J. Malone and another man, Joseph Evans a.k.a. Kane, a reputed member of a Queens based drug gang. Police don't know if the Malone-Evans murders are somehow related to several other murders earlier, involving a police detective...."

Vita slipped smoothly and gently out of the bed, glancing over her shoulder at a snoring Baby Wise. She grabbed her Blackberry off the nightstand then headed into the living room naked. She began to text a message:

> Damn Bacardi ain't bullshittin' huh? One down three to go! LOL

Antoinette looked at her iPhone and peeped the text with a smile. She inhaled a blunt she was smoking then text back:

> ...if he only knew, huh? This shit is 2 easy!

Vita sat on the couch, Indian style and replied.

Our team abt 2 b RICH!

Antoinette heard Biz get up in the bedroom. She erased Vita's messages, put down her phone and grabbed a glass and filling it with soda.

"Baby, you okay? You want somethin' to drink?" she asked seductively, carrying the glass to the bedroom for him. She was playing her position to the tee.

3:00 A.M.
HALLOWEEN

Autumn rolled over in the bed to find Bacardi wasn't there. She pushed her hair out of her face and got up, wearing one of Bacardi's t-shirts. She walked into the living room to find him looking at the television with the sound turned down. On screen she saw the CNN logo and a scene of some war in the Middle East. He sat quietly, a drink in one hand, a pre-paid burn out in his other. On the coffee table in front of him was a humongous .357 automatic. Autumn came up behind him and began massaging his shoulders. "I must be losin' my touch," she joked. "After a shot like that you 'posed to be sleep."

Bacardi laughed lightly then kissed her hand, using that same hand to lead her around the couch and onto his lap.

"Naw baby, you know you got that snapper. Shit just tense right now, gotta be on my P's and Q's."

"I know love. I was just messin' with you. You okay though?"

Bacardi sipped his drink and nodded.

"Just sittin' here watchin' the news. J. Malone got killed."

"Are you fucking kidding me?" she asked, surprised.

"Damn, what happened?" she continued.

"Nigga got gunned down at his own party," he shrugged. Then added, "Fuck it. He wanted to be a gangsta so bad, you play wit' fire, you get burned."

He didn't tell her that it was him that sent the hit on Kane at the party, and that he had just received a call telling him to watch the news. When he found out J. Malone was one of the six people killed he felt no remorse for J was just a casualty of war.

For Autumn, she already knew the deal and he didn't have to tell her. She knew if he was watching the news he was somehow involved. She kept her mouth shut though. She could tell he just needed to talk, so she just listened.

"Yo... you know how long I've been knowin' Baby Wise? Practically came up wit' this nigga. I mean, he from the Southside, but he was never on that Southside/Hollis bullshit. His man Kane was but he ain't never come at me side ways. Fuck em'," he remarked, picturing them in his mind, his brains all over J. Malone. "But me and Baby Wise, word up, anybody in Queens, anybody but Baby Wise and I coulda' seen this coming. This nigga's head is fucked up. He ain't even looking at the obvious."

"What's that?" Autumn asked curiously.

Bacardi looked at her.

"This shit ain't no beef, somebody done set us both up," he sneered. "Whoever did it, knew shit was goin' down and robbed us. But something or somebody got this nigga thinkin' I flipped on him! Fuck outta here," he said now pacing. "And this nigga, Baby Wise, he ain't thinking straight. He was always an emotional nigga, even in fucking high school, you couldn't say nothing to this nigga without his fucking face cracking into a thousand pieces," he shook his head.

"You say somebody, but you got an idea who it is, don't you? You think Biz had something to do with it, huh?"

85

Autumn questioned slyly.

Bacardi smiled a crooked grin.

"Biz was fuckin' Renee."

"Owens?"

"Yeah, he think I ain't know, but come on yo, I got eyes in the back of my head," he boasted.

Let me find out this nigga was fuckin' her too. But Autumn had learned to keep her feelings in check. She let the comment fly by.

"So, maybe he got in her head. Found out what room they were in, because only she knew. I kept it that way, never use the same room twice, feel me? That way a nigga can't know in advance. Then after that, bam," he aimed his finger like a gun, "No more Renee once the smoke clears. He claims to have found the niggas who did it. The same niggas he used in the first place!" he chuckled. "But now it's a beef with me and Baby Wise. If we kill each other, whose gonna be the man in Queens?"

Autumn nodded, seeing his point.

"So, that's why you want me to get at Antoinette."

"Exactly, get in the bitch head. Tell her how many other bitches he fuckin'...make her see light at the end of the tunnel," he replied.

Autumn kissed him gently.

"Say no more, baby. I got you."

"I know," he answered, embracing her. "That's why I love you."

"You better!" she giggled, slowly dropping to her knees.

8:30 A.M.
HALLOWEEN

The knock at the door was answered almost immediately by Face. He didn't even peep through the peephole. He didn't have to. Antoinette had already called and let him know she was on her way. He had been watching out the window and saw her pull up. He wanted to make sure she had come alone. If not, he knew shit would get messy. It had already been decided that Antoinette wouldn't leave the building alive. He didn't want to have to murder whoever was with her in broad daylight also, but if shit came to that, then so be it. So, when he saw she was alone, he was relieved. A few minutes later came the knock on the door.

"Hey baby," she greeted him cheerfully, wrapping her arms around his neck and tonguing him down.

He kissed her back, but there was something about his kiss, something missing. It was then that her instinct told her what was wrong. He planned to do to her what she came to do to him and the others. She instantly got on point. She put her hands in the coat pocket of the waist length fox fur and subtly scanned the apartment. The fact that Tank was sitting on the couch, was something she didn't miss.

"Where is Bop and Mellow?" she asked.

"They went to get the van," Face told her, unable to meet her eyes.

This nigga don't want to do it, Antoinette thought,

assessing the situation.

"Well, where's my money at?' she asked with a smile.

"In the back, ma. I got you," Face assured her.

"Money on the wood makes the game go good," she cracked with a wink. "I gotta get back before Biz misses me.'

"No doubt, yo, Mellow'll be here any minute. I'll get the dough," Face said, then headed to the back.

Antoinette's mind was working overtime. She figured they might get on some Brooklyn bullshit and try and kill her. But, she had relied on the fact that Face was feeling her and wouldn't let it go down like that. It was obvious that she was wrong and that wasn't the case, so it was good that all four weren't there. She knew she had to do something before the other two got back. Her window was closing.

Her eyes followed Face in the back, then fell on Tank who was looking at her.

"Why you lookin' at me like that?" Antoinette asked, in a half joking manner. Tank was making her nervous.

"Lookin' at you like what?" he retorted, grilling her.

"All crazy and shit."

"Maybe I'm crazy."

She rolled her eyes at him. *Whatever nigga, I got your crazy.*

Face came back carrying five large stacks of money and set them on the table.

"Hundred large, ma. I told you I got you," Face winked.

The tension seemed so thick, it was buzzing in Antoinette's ears. She saw that Face wasn't armed, but a Mac 11 lay on the coffee table in front of where Tank was sitting. Her mind screamed do it! Adrenaline rushed through her nerve endings. It was now or never. Hit Tank's ass first then Face.

"Hold up, I forgot something," she mumbled, turning for the door. At the same time she cocked the .38 snub nose in her pocket and in one smooth motion, spun around like a Ninja aiming her gun straight for Tank.

"I knew that bitch wa..." was all Tank got out before the shit caught him in the chest. As he leaned forward to pick up the Mac on the table, the force slammed him back against the couch.

"Stinkin' bitch!" Face barked, thinking he was close enough to grab Antoinette. Just as he grabbed her free hand she put the gun point blank to his heart.

Boom! Boom!

His eyes popped wide then she saw the light go out in them. His dead weight leaned against her. She kissed his lips and whispered, "I got you, too, baby," then shoved him off her and watched him hit the floor. When she looked back at Tank, she was surprised to see him struggling to aim the Mac at her.

Boom!

Boom! Boom! Boom!

He shot at her, then she shot at him, emptying the chamber in him, hitting him in the neck, cheek and left eye. His shot was a flesh wound that tore through her abdominal section setting her on fire and in exacerbating pain. She hit the ground landing on Face.

"Fuck!" she growled, rocking back and forth in pain. *Get up,* she urged herself, knowing she had to blow the scene. Using the armchair as leverage, she pulled herself up and put the empty gun in her pocket. Antoinette looked at the money on the table. A split second was all it took for her to decide between leaving with or without it. Her greed won out and it was precisely that greed that saved her life.

Bop and Mellow were back, had just parked the MPV, turned off the ignition and the loud ass rap music of Lil' Wayne, just in time to hear the three shots that ended Tank's existence. "What the fuck!" Bop cursed.

He and Mellow jumped out of the car, pistols drawn, heading for the building. Meanwhile, inside, Antoinette had grabbed the duffle bag off the bed and headed for the door.

She didn't even look twice at the stack on the table. She couldn't waste anymore time, but she did grab the Mac out of Tanks dead hands. Limping, she quickly fled the apartment, leaving the door open as she headed down the stairs.

That's why her greed saved her life.

Had she not took the time to get the money and instead went straight out the door she would've been in the stair case with Bop and Mellow at the same time. She would've been a sitting duck.

But because she was delayed, she had just turned the landing when Bop peeped her and peeped the duffle bag and shot at her, just missing her head.

"Shit!" she cursed, taking the Mac with both hands and fired blindly around the landing corner causing Bop and Mellow to scatter for cover.

She turned back to the corridor and banged on the first door she saw.

"Open up, I'm shot," she banged.

"No here! No home!" the feminine Latin voice yelled back.

"Fuck this," she growled, stepped back and let the Mac rip, aiming for the lock.

The women inside screamed as Antoinette shouldered her way inside, just as Bop and Mellow sparked the door sill.

"Don't kill me!" the women begged, cowering in the corner.

"Tell them that," Antoinette shot back, shooting as she backed her way down the apartment hallway. She saw the fire escape outside of the bedroom window and headed for it. She grabbed the lamp off the table and smashed the window with it.

"Downstairs! Go downstairs!" Mellow told Bop, anticipating Antoinette's next move as Bop headed for the stairs.

Mellow pushed deeper in the apartment cautiously. When he saw the busted window he ran to it, and looked down. He could see Antoinette descending the fire escape through the metal gratings. There was no way he could hit her as she was protected by the fire escape itself.

"You dead bitch!" he barked, running out of the room.

Antoinette dropped the last few feet to ground level from the ladder in front of the building. People on the sidewalk marveled as Antoinette passed out from the lost of blood.

"Look at the woman."

"Yo, shortie hit!"

"What the fuck!"

When Bop came out he saw the crowd of people around Antoinette. There was no way he was walking up in that crowd. By the time Mellow came down, Bop was already in his blue Escalade, engine running.

"Nigga, come on!" Bop urged.

Mellow looked at the crowd only a half a block away. He was tempted, but a cop car was coming down the street and that made his mind up for him.

"Fuck!" he barked, then hopped in the car as Bop drove away.

9:00 A.M.
HALLOWEEN

"Yo Grip, Grip, come on B, not my man," Baby Wise intoned, holding back tears Vita had never seen in his eyes before.

She knew then that Kane was dead.

"Yo, Baby Wise, I'm sayin..." Grip replied sadly, although his sadness was generated by guilt. "I can't believe this shit."

Damn, that niggas a fuckin' snake, Wise thought to himself.

Baby Wise sat down on the couch, his forehead cradled in the palm of his right hand and the phone in his left.

"When?" Baby Wise wanted to know.

"Malone's party in Manhattan last night," Grip answered. "We got the cocksucka who did it though."

"No you didn't"

"Huh?"

"I said," Baby Wise seethed, "No you didn't. But I will...I swear on Kane's grave I will."

The steel in his tone sent a slight chill through Grip. He knew if Baby Wise ever found out that he was the one who set Kane up, his death would be slow and painful, all the more reason in Grip's mind to make sure that didn't happen.

"No doubt my dude, I'm wit' you on that. Shit gonna get handled! But yo, I need to holla at you, where you at? I'm comin' through."

"Nah," Baby Wise replied off handedly, like his mind wasn't completely on the conversation, "I'll hit you later, dunn...this shit is crazy."

The phone went dead in Grip's car, so he lowered it to his lap.

"What he say? He tell you where he at?" Biz quizzed him seated next to Grip in his Mercedes Benz and they drove down Hillside Avenue.

Grip shook his head.

"Nah, but we need to find him," Grip replied, a subtle nervousness in his tone.

Biz found it amusing, but suppressed his smile.

"No doubt, Dunn, we will."

"Today," said Grip in a boisterous tone.

Biz snickered.

"Just chill yo, that nigga don't know what's goin' on."

"Yo, son, I'm sayin', now Kane dead he's gonna be on a rampage," Grip remarked. "That was Wise's man."

Snake ass nigga, don't get shook now. Biz thought to himself. *Bacardi shoulda let me murder this faggot!*

But Biz already knew Bacardi wouldn't have Grip killed. Bacardi was a man of his word so when he told Grip he was going to put him in Baby Wise's position, he meant it. For Bacardi, it was a way of keeping balance in the street. Grip knew Baby Wise's organization inside out, so he was in the best position to keep it running. Besides, Grip was weak and easy to control...a puppet on Bacardi's string.

But, Biz had other plans. If anybody deserved Baby Wise's blocks and position, he felt it was him. Bacardi acted like he wanted to keep Biz under him, not let him branch out. But Biz wasn't having it, so once the smoke cleared he'd take care of Grip himself that was his plan.

Wise flipped his phone closed and laid it on the table Vita had been watching him throughout his conversation.

"Baby, you okay?" she asked, coming up behind him sitting on the couch and massage his shoulders.

"Kane," was all he would say.

A slight smile crept across Vitas lips but Baby Wise never saw it. Instead he felt her arms wrap around him and then she said, "Oh my God, baby! Kane! What happened?

Baby Wise explained almost word for word what Grip had told him about Kane's murder.

"What about the dudes you said was with Kane What did they say?" she asked playing the role of concerned girlfriend.

"Grip just told me, yo. I ain't had a chance to talk to 'em."

"I know that. I mean what Grip say they said? Didn' he talk to 'em? And why wasn't he there, too? Him and Kane always together. What about Malone's party? That shit's bigger than Puff's parties. It ain't like Grip was gonna miss that," Vita insinuated, recognizing another opportunity to get in Baby Wise's head and cloud his vision.

He stood, pinching his bottom lip pensively.

"Yeah, true....I'ma definitely holla at him about that Why wasn't he there? Fuck! Yo, Vita, fix me something to eat while I make this call."

"Baby, its nothin' here," she informed him glancing at her watch. "But I can go grab something from the store."

"Naw ma, I'll take care of it. Just let me make this call real quick."

"Go head Wise, handle your B.I. I gotta get back to

Queens anyway to get my hair..."

Baby Wise looked at her sharply.

"I don't want you in Queens right now."

"Bu..."

Baby Wise stood up and gently caressed her cheek.

"No buts, Vita. Shit is too serious. I already lost my nigga. I'm not losing you," he shook his head and the look she saw in his eyes sent shivers down her spine, "I'll kill every nigga in Queens, braveheart, ya heard."

For a moment, Vita was overwhelmed with the depth of Baby Wise's love. She knew he was sincere. But her head won the argument with her heart because, he may have loved her, but his love came with a fist.

Stay focused, she told herself.

"Okay, daddy, whatever you say," she said, submissively.

He kissed her then grabbed his keys.

"What you want?" he asked.

"Surprise me."

Baby Wise walked out the door. Vita snatched up her phone and called Antoinette. Something was wrong. She could feel it. Antoinette should've called by now. Vita knew that Antoinette was going over to handle Face and his crew. *Damn, please tell me everything went smooth, please tell me she knocked those niggas and we're straight. Please, please, please, no fuck ups.*

Her phone went straight to voicemail.

"Shit!" Vita cursed then took a deep breath and made one more call...

9:17 A.M.
HALLOWEEN

"Recognize him?" Detective Wilcox asked, sliding a picture across his desk to Rahjohn.

The three of them were sitting in Wilcox's office.

"Of course, that's Kane, Baby Wise's right hand man," Rahjohn answered, handing the picture to Natasha.

Well, for now on, Baby Wise is left handed because as of approximately three a.m. he is known as the deceased."

Rahjohn followed, "So, Bacardi went right for the jugular, huh?"

"That ain't all," Wilcox quipped.

Wilcox brought them up to speed on the shootout at J. Malone's party. Besides Malone and Kane, several others were shot, including a well-known R&B singer who would be paralyzed from the neck down.

"Wow," Natasha remarked, "Play with fire, huh?"

"The only problem, we're the ones getting burned," Wilcox huffed. "Again, the media's having' a field day on top of the dirty cop angle, now we've got prominent members of the Hip Hop community with toe tags and wheelchairs! I'm going to put you in touch with the detectives in Harlem that's working on the case, god damn Hip Hop police."

Rahjohn nodded, then he explained everything he and Natasha had learned, and the theory they were going on.

"I don't like theories," Wilcox grumbled, "because

there are no theoretical murders. Get me facts dammit!"

"Well, what little facts we have point in this direction. Once we get Renee Owen's phone records back, we'll be in a better position to know," Natasha explained.

Wilcox sipped his coffee then said, "I'm not saying you guys are wrong, I'm saying you better be right! If this is a robbery situation then the best thing to do is get Baby Wise and Bacardi off the streets while we find out who did it."

"On what grounds?" Rahjohn probed. "These guys can afford some helluva mouth pieces. They'll have 'em back on the street in no time and it'll all make the evening news some how."

"Let me take care of that," Wilcox assured him. "The Mayor's watching' this closely so whatever strings he has to pull or chains he has to yank, he'll make it happen."

Rahjohn's phone rang.

"Yeah," he answered.

"What do you want for Christmas?" Detective Little snickered.

"That, my friend, may be too much for your virgin ears to take," Rahjohn joked. "Why, what've you got?"

Natasha was all in it. "Who's that?"

Rahjohn held up his pointer finger, to hold her down.

"Shootout in East New York, two dead and a woman in the hospital."

"And? What's new? It sounds like a typical day in Brooklyn to me," Rahjohn cracked.

"Yeah, it would be if the chick in question wasn't trying to make off with half a million and the cops found a certain burgundy MPV we had an APB out on," Little explained.

Rahjohn's ears perked up.

"My MPV?"

"Merry fucking Christmas! Sometimes shit just happens, dude. Shit just happens," Little said sounding like he was humming a tune instead of actually speaking.

"Which hospital?"

"King's County Hospital, East Brooklyn."

"I'm on it," Rahjohn responded, hung up then said to Natasha, "They found the MPV in Brooklyn."

They both stood up.

"Brooklyn?!" Wilcox growled then sighed hard. "If this keeps up, every fuckin' Borough in New York'll be involved!"

Rahjohn and Natasha exited the office, as Wilcox downed his coffee in one gulp, wishing it was something stronger.

9:23 AM
HALLOWEEN

Grip put himself in Baby Wise's shoes, thinking what would be his next move if he was Baby Wise. It didn't take long for him to figure it out. He explained the situation to Biz, then dropped him off and headed for Guy R. Brewer Boulevard, where he knew he'd find Kane's young guns.

To Grip, it was simple. He figured if he was Baby Wise, the first thing Baby Wise would do, would be to talk to somebody that was there. Of course, he wouldn't want to talk about it over the phone, and he'd want to meet up, talk in person. Grip needed to find out where Baby Wise would want Kane's young guns to meet him. Once he discovered this fact, all he had to do was let Biz know so they could handle it. He definitely wasn't doing it himself.

One Sixteenth to 120th and Guy R. Brewer used to be a Supreme Team spot in the eighties, but Baby Wise had converted it into a heroin spot. The heaviest traffic came in the mornings, when junkies needed to get the monkey off their back, and at night the spot was so busy it looked like they were giving away free cheese. This is how Grip knew he could find Kane's people because, like addicts, block huggers are predictable too.

He slowly crept through the block doing two miles an hour in the non-descript '01 Honda Accord he used when he was being incognito. He spotted one of the dudes.

"Yo, K.K.!"

The young dude, no more than eighteen and one hundred and forty pounds, snatched the Desert Eagle from his pants and started to aim.

"Yo K, It's me! Grip!" Grip barked, hitting the brakes.

"Grip," K.K. squinted, cigarette hanging out of his mouth. "Nigga, you better identify yo' motherfuckin' self. You know shit is on, Dunn."

"Where Dick-Dick?"

"Up the block. What up?" K.K. wanted to know.

"Come on, get in."

K.K. wasn't the type to ask questions. He just acted. He got in and gave Grip dap.

"Yo dunn, they kilt 'em man, they got my muhfuckin' man," K.K. hissed.

"Yeah yo, I'm fucked up."

"Shit can't go unanswered"

"No doubt...yo Dick-Dick! Come on Nigga, ride wit me!" Grip yelled out the window.

Dick-Dick got off the milk crate and started for the bushes.

"Naw yo, you don't need that. Just come on!"

Dick-Dick got in the back seat and they pulled off. K.K. and Dick Dick were both wild and animated, so they gave Grip a blow by blow description of what happened at J. Malone's party, and how they busted their guns.

"He killed Smoke too?"

"Yeah, God bless the dead, fuckin' lifted him and blew his fuckin' guts all over me, Dunn!" Dick-Dick exclaimed.

"Fo sho, but we blasted right through the faggot Malone 'til we stretched that bitch nigga, 'cause he was usin' Malone like a shield.

Grip rode for a minute, then said, "Baby Wise holla at y'all yet?"

100

"Yeah, we 'bout to go meet him in a minute," K.K. replied.

"Where?"

Sometimes, one word is all it takes, one wrong answer, or one too many questions, and if you in the game balls deep and you on point, that's all it takes to set your street senses to fortify. So when Grip asked, "Where?" K.K. mentally questioned the inquiry, not because he distrusted Grip, but because there was no logical reason for him to ask. So K.K. answered evasively.

"What, you ain't talk to him yet?" K.K. answered him evasively with a question instead of an answer.

"Yeah, yeah, I hollered at him earlier, but I was just sayin', you know, tell me where and I'll take you now, "Grip stumbled slightly over his words.

To K.K., he seemed pressed to know, which gave K.K. more resolve to not tell him.

"Nah Dunn, we good. Plus, he ain't even tell us where yet," K.K. lied.

Grip chuckled as he pulled over along a desolate stretch of Guy R. Brewer Boulevard.

"Come on K, how you gonna meet him if you don't know where?"

"Won't you just call him yourself," Dick-Dick spoke up from the back seat.

Grip's eyes shot him daggers through the rearview mirror.

"Yeah.... No doubt," Grip replied. "I'll do that now."

He reached in his pocket like he was reaching for his phone, but in actuality, his phone was in the other pocket, therefore his hand was really gripping his gun.

Grip couldn't call Baby Wise because his guilty conscience wouldn't let him. He felt like Baby Wise would think he was prying, and it would make him suspicious. Then instead of Grip setting Baby Wise up, Baby Wise would be waiting on him.

He hadn't planned on killing the young boys, but he hadn't planned on them being on point like that either. How could they not tell him? But in their minds, how could he not know? And if he didn't' know it meant Baby Wise hadn't told him and if Baby Wise hadn't told him, why should they?

Grip definitely didn't want to kill them but his hand was forced when his phone rang. K.K. caught on instantly, because the sounds of his 50 cent ringtone was coming out of his right pocket, but Grip's hand was in his left.

What the fuck is this nigga reaching for? K.K. thought. When Grip saw K.K. reaching in the wrong pocket he had no choice but to pull his pistol and put it to K.K.'s chin.

"Yo Grip, what the fuck?!" Dick-Dick barked confusedly.

"Shut the fuck up! You move and I splatter your man!" Grip growled, taking K.K.'s gun off him.

"Yo Grip man, you buggin', Dunn," Dick-Dick remarked because he didn't see it, but K.K. did.

"Naw Dick, this shit make perfect sense," K.K. sneered, looking Grip dead in the eye. "That's why this nigga ain't come to the party last night... and that's why he wanna know where Baby Wise at now, this nigga suckin' Bacardi dick."

Grip pushed the gun hard into K.K.'s neck, making him bump his head against the window.

"Say it again nigga! I..."

That's all Grip got out before Dick-Dick caught him dead in the jaw with a hard right that dazed Grip and rocked him back in his seat. The two young guns knew they were going to die, so there was nothing to lose and Dick-Dick seized the initiative.

When the first blow landed, K.K. wasted no time in getting involved. He launched a blow that broke Grip's nose on contact, causing blood to run from it like someone had turned on a faucet.

But Grip had the gun, so even though their fight was valiant, it ended for K.K. when Grip pulled the trigger twice and blew K.K.'s brains all over the car ceiling and passenger seat.

"I'ma kill you!" Dick-Dick huffed, wrapping his arm around Grip's neck and pinning his head against the headrest. Dick-Dick was now sitting behind Grip, so Grip couldn't shoot him easily. He had to use one hand to try to loosen the choke hold Dick-Dick had on him. Feeling woozy, Grip aimed the gun under his arm and put it to the seat.

Boom!

"Aarrghh!" Dick-Dick bellowed, feeling the bullet tear through his rib cage.

Boom!

The second shot through the seat buckled Dick-Dick and made him release Grip. Fumbling and holding his gushing rib cage, he managed to tumble out of the car. Grip, gasping for air and coughing, got out in pursuit of Dick-Dick. He pulled his shirt collar up over his mouth and nose to conceal his identity then aimed his gun at Dick-Dick who had stumbled to the curb.

"Bi-Bitch ass nigga! Yous a snake ass nigga, Grip," Dick-Dick cursed and Grip replied with two shots to the dome, leaving him dead in the street.

Grip ran around the front of the vehicle and pulled K.K.'s body out of the car. He jumped in, lowering the passenger side window because of the blood all over it. K.K.'s brain matter and blood gathered at the base of the window, as Grip pulled off with screeching tires. His adrenaline was pumping so hard, he could hear his heart beating in his ears. All he was thinking about was torching the car, and he forgot all about the fact that his phone had rang.

103

10:11 A.M.
HALLOWEEN

Antoinette was still a little weak from the loss of blood, and a little high from the medication, but she was still her vibrant self when Rahjohn and Natasha walked in.

"Damn, I hope you my doctor," she remarked, eyeing Rahjohn brazenly, one eyebrow arched.

He flashed his badge.

"Naw baby, Detective Griffin."

"What a shame," she replied, turning her head away, and closing her eyes.

"I could say the same about you," Rahjohn smirked. "Pretty girl like you getting mixed up in ugly things like murder, robbery... drugs."

"Like I told them other dicks..." using the abbreviated form of detective with a derogatory meaning, "I'm a victim of a stray bullet. I don't know who did it."

Natasha snickered.

"Stray bullet, huh? So you just happened to be walking by a place where two men were killed with three hundred and fifty dollars in a book bag and bam! Stray bullet?"

Antoinette's mind laughed to itself. There was four hundred thousand in the bag, which meant the police took a fifty thousand dollar finder's fee. Everyone was dirty in the game.

"Guess it ain't my day," Antoinette retorted, eyeing Natasha in a standoffish manner.

"Definitely not, when the gun in your pocket matches the bullets in both victims," Rahjohn told her.

Antoinette laughed then grimaced because of a pain that shot through her stomach.

"Yeah right, ballistics don't come back that fast."

Rahjohn chuckled amused by the fact that Antoinette called his bluff.

"Oh, I see. This isn't your first time on this ride, huh?" he remarked, sitting down in the chair by the bed. "But what about when they do come back? We know you were in that building. And you made your escape through a woman's apartment that you blew the lock off of. You're a soldier, I'll say that. But, in this war, you may be outgunned."

Antoinette looked him in the eye solemnly then took a deep breath.

"So, I guess you want me to tell you," she smiled seductively staring in his eyes.

"It can only help in the long run."

"Okay, I'ma tell you," she said then looked at Rahjohn, "that I don't have on any panties under this robe, wanna see?" she winked.

Rahjohn leaned back in the chair with a smile that said, 'you got me'.

"That's not what we're talking about," he said adjusting himself back into detective mode determined to be about his job.

"Well, it's what I'm talking about. Anything else, I want a lawyer for," Antoinette shot back.

"So you wanna play games?" Natasha said, standing over on the opposite side. "You think murder's a game? We know you ain't in this alone, so why don't you make it light on yourself."

Antoinette looked at Natasha as if she was crazy then back at Rahjohn.

"Yo... she can't be serious?"

Rahjohn stood up, subtly shaking his head at Natasha.

"She wants a lawyer, let her have her lawyer. We're done here. But, hey listen Antoinette... I know the 'no snitching' rule is in effect here, but you know, New York reinstated the death penalty... and a few years from now, when you're taking that last walk and the people you're protecting ain't come to see you or sent you a dime... all that hood shit is gonna look pretty fuckin' stupid."

Antoinette pushed back the covers, pulled up her hospital gown and spread her legs, revealing her cleanly shaven peach.

"Ain't it pretty? If it was a dick, I'd tell you to suck it," she hissed then kissed the air.

"We'll be in touch," Rahjohn retorted.

When Rahjohn and Natasha came out, they overheard two uniformed officers assigned to guard Antoinette talking to someone.

"I'm sorry Miss, but she's in custody so she can't have any visitors."

"But she's my friend. I just wanna make sure she's okay."

Rahjohn stepped around the officers and saw that it was Autumn.

"What's going on?" he asked the officers, then to her, "Autumn, right? What are you doing here?"

"I just wanted to make sure Antoinette was okay," she replied.

"How do you know her, may I ask?" Natasha questioned her.

Autumn answered but she was looking at Rahjohn.

"Through a friend who knows Biz, is she okay?"

"Yeah, physically but she's in a lot of trouble," Rahjohn told her.

"What happened?"

"I'm sorry. I can't discuss that."

"I understand... But if I could see her for myself," Autumn inquired.

Rahjohn and Natasha exchanged glances then Rahjohn gestured for Autumn to move over to the side so that he could speak with her.

"I'll let you in on one condition. You tell me everything you know about what's going on Between Bacardi and Baby Wise."

"I don't know what's going on, detective."

"Rahjohn."

She smiled demurely.

"Rahjohn?"

"Now come on ma, this thing is getting real ugly. These two seem bent on killing each other, and you could be right in the line of fire. I know you wanna talk to me," he said, remembering the look she gave him at the club.

Autumn considered it, sighed the replied, "Okay, but not here, not now."

"When?"

"Give me your number. I'll call you at noon," she told him, but when he looked at her skeptically, she added with a smile, "I promise. I will."

"You're asking a lot of me."

"You're asking a lot of me, too," she shot back. "Do you know what Bacardi will do to me if he finds out I'm talking to you?"

Rahjohn considered her point then said, "Okay... noon. And don't make me chase you, because I will find you," he said, without a smile on his face, but flirtation in his tone.

"Don't make promises you can't keep," she winked,

going around him.

Rahjohn turned back to the officers.

"Okay guys, escort her in and give her fifteen minutes."

One of the officers replied, "Sorry detective, but that's not your decision."

"I'll take the weight, okay? Fifteen minutes, and you'll be there the whole time. No big deal."

The officers looked at each other then relented.

"You'll take the weight?"

"Taken."

"Famous last words," the other officer quipped as he escorted Autumn inside.

Rahjohn said a few words to the remaining officer, who nodded his agreement then Rahjohn and Natasha left.

"We need to put a tail on her."

"Why?"

"That's the quickest way to find Bacardi, you think?" Natasha replied sarcastically, stating the obvious.

"And?" Rahjohn probed, glancing at her as he drove. He sensed there was more to her suggestion.

"Maybe she's connected to the remaining two guys involved in the robbery."

"So you think she's involved?"

"She made herself a suspect when she came to the hospital," Natasha surmised.

Rahjohn struggled with the thought.

"Maybe, or maybe it is just what she said it is. She was just visiting a friend."

"Well, she'd have to be a pretty special friend to go through all she went through just to see her," Natasha signified.

Rahjohn caught her implications, and laughed. "Nah,

I doubt that."

"Yeah, you would."

He stopped at the light and looked at her.

"Are we still talking about the case?" he asked

Natasha sucked her teeth.

"Please, Rahjohn. Everything is not about you, okay? All I said is we should have her tailed. You're the one with all the answers, like she's above reproach or something."

"Did I say that?" He shot back, defensive because of what he felt she was implying. "I'm just playing devil's advocate, so we don't waste our time chasing dead ends."

The light greened and they pulled off, both remaining silent, because they were scared any word could be used against them emotionally. After a short, tense void, Natasha broke the forming ice with a soft chuckle.

"What's so funny?" Rahjohn asked.

"I was just thinking." She continued chuckling, "If it's a boy, I'm getting him neutered from the jump. I'll be damn if I raise another you!"

They both laughed, as they entered the borough of Queens.

"So, it's official?" Rahjohn inquired.

"I don't believe in abortions, your donated demon sperm included."

"Neither do I," Rahjohn replied with a smile. "This is our bed we've made... literally."

"Rahjohn..." she began, wanting to tell him how relieved she was to know that he wanted her to have his child, to tell him how happy, how full she felt carrying a part of him inside of her, tell him that no matter what, no one could love him like she did and that she would be there for him no matter what until her dying day. But she couldn't. She was afraid he'd use her love against her. Natasha didn't want him to know he had that kind of power over her, so she simply added as if he didn't have to hear her, "I still think we should have had her tailed."

His smile told her he knew she wanted to say something else, but he didn't pursue it. Instead he winked and replied, "What do you think I was telling that officer before we left?"

10:45 A.M.
HALLOWEEN

The sounds of Alicia Keys' *No One* filled Autumn's burgundy Benz E550. She drummed her slender, manicured fingers on the steering wheel while casually glancing in her rearview mirror, smiling to herself. It amused her to think that the police thought she didn't see them. Somebody should've told the two Italian-looking white boys she was from the Bridges 41st side and could spot a cop a mile away. Beside, Bacardi had taught her to always be aware of her surroundings.

"If you make three turns in any direction and the same car is behind you, it's not a coincidence, it's a setup, ya heard? Pay attention."

And that's exactly what this was. When she had noticed them, she decided not to head for Harlem. She didn't want them to know where they were really at, so she led them to Queens where they thought she would go. Autumn reached for her phone to call Bacardi, but didn't know if her phone was tapped, so she decided against it.

Her thoughts turned to Rahjohn. She knew he was the reason behind all this, but she wasn't mad at him. She expected no less. Her only concerns with him were if he really wanted to help her and if she could trust him. She envisioned their conversation over and over again. He seemed sincere enough and she could tell he liked her just by the way he stared at her. Something about him attracted her, but she knew it was out of the question. Besides, Bacardi would never give her up without a fight.

She also couldn't help to wonder if Rahjohn would fight for her freedom, as hard as he would fight to take Bacardi's away. That was the one question she intended to find the answer to.

Autumn pulled into the parking lot of the Coliseum, Queens' famous fashion bazaar slash mall. She checked to see that the police unmarked was still with her then parked, got out and chirped the alarm.

When she got inside, she cut over by the phone booths, waiting to see if they'd pursue on foot as well.

They didn't.

"Piece of cake," she thought to herself, heading for the boutique. When she got there, the saleswoman, a short but buxom Boricua, looked up from her customer and smiled, "What's up Autumn, girl? I'll be right with you."

True to her word, she excused herself from her customer and came over to Autumn, giving her a hug.

"Maria, I need your car," Autumn stated bluntly, handing her the keys to her own car and wanting Maria's in return.

Maria wasn't insulted by her bluntness, she simply replied, "Is everything okay?" she asked smiling at the small black Mercedes Benz car key.

Maria had already heard of the beef between Bacardi and Baby Wise, so Maria assumed Autumn was in a bind, which she was. But since she was also her girl and Autumn was driving a Mercedes and she wasn't, it was no questions asked.

Maria grabbed her purse from behind the counter and dug out her keys.

"You still pushing the yellow 'Vette?" Autumn asked, accepting the keys.

"Yes, with the 'Maria' plates, second parking deck. Can't miss it. You still got the Burgundy E Class, right?"

Autumn nodded.

"I'll hit you later so we can meet up."

"Handle your biz, mami," Maria snickered as Autumn walked out.

As Autumn pulled out in the Corvette, she noticed the two officers eating hot dogs in the car and still watching her Benz.

"Holla," she giggled, as she pulled off.

"What car you done stole?" Bacardi asked.

Autumn wrapped her arms around his neck and sucked his bottom lip.

"It's Maria's. I ran into a little problem. The cops followed me from the hospital."

"Yeah?" he replied, glancing out of the living room window, reflexively.

"Don't worry," Autumn assured him, sitting on the couch. "They're probably still in the Coliseum parking lot," she snickered.

"So, shorty in the hospital, huh?" he probed, sitting beside her.

Autumn nodded.

"And under heavy police presence; I almost didn't get in but... that detective was there."

"Who, Griffin, in Brooklyn? Fuck he doin' in Brooklyn, that ain't his watch," Bacardi remarked.

Autumn shrugged an 'I don't know'.

"But if it wasn't for him, I woulda never got in to see

her."

Bacardi looked at her.

"Yeah? What you promise him?"

Bacardi knew police don't give up anything without reciprocation, so there was no need to lie to him even if Autumn wanted to.

"He wanted me to talk to him about you, but you know I gave the 'gimme your number' bit. But you know, that's dead," she replied, telling him the truth but not her real intention. "I'm not calling his ass."

Bacardi nodded.

"So what up with shorty? You get the feeling she talkin'? You get in her head?"

Autumn shook her head.

"I couldn't. There was a cop there the whole time, but I did leave her my number. If Biz does have somethin' to do with this and that's why Antoinette got shot, then he definitely ain't on her good side right now," Autumn surmised.

Bacardi got up, pacing the floor.

"Damn man, I wonder what the fuck happened? Shit gotta be connected...." He paced to the window and back, and then turned to her. "You said Griffin got you in?"

"Yeah."

Bacardi smirked.

"He feelin' you. I saw it last night at the club. Ai-ight look, holla at the nigga. Tell him..."

"Hold up, you want me to talk to the police?" she asked, with more indignation than she was actually feeling.

"Like I always tell you, baby, this chess, not checkers. You can get at this dude and find out what he knows. Make him work for us without him knowing, you feel me? He might already know who did this or maybe even where Baby Wise at. Bottom line ma, work the nigga."

"So... you don't want me to... have sex with him?"

Autumn asked, getting her mandate clear.

Whatever it take, he thought diabolically, but said, "Naw, baby, hell no," he said knowing he couldn't tell his baby girl he wanted her to do that. "Just... make it do what it do when you do what you does," he snickered.

Autumn smiled.

"I get you, baby."

It couldn't have worked out better if she'd planned it herself.

10:50 A.M.
HALLOWEEN

All Grip could think at the moment was, *Goddamn, I know why that nigga married you.* He was laid back in his bedroom on his massive waterbed, enjoying the oral pleasures of his next door neighbor's wife. If her husband would've been home, Grip imagined he could hear him fucking her through the apartment wall.

"Yeah, you nasty bitch. Suck that dick ...umph!" Grip moaned, palming the back of her blond weave.

She wasn't that bad on the eyes, but she wasn't that attractive either. She was a little on the plump side. But girlfriend was a straight certified nympho that took it anyway you could give it. Grip wasn't the only one in the building she was fucking. He knew it too.

The harder he forced his shaft down her throat, the more turned on she got, fingering her self with four fingers vigorously.

"I'm 'bout to cum baby! You gonna swallow cum for daddy?" Grip grunted.

"Mm hmmm," she mumbled mouth full of dick.

"Huh?"

"Hmmm mmm."

Grip released his load deep down her throat, and true

to her word, she didn't regurgitate. She swallowed and sucked him until she milked him dry.

"Come on baby, mama wanna cum again," she panted, turning around and tooting her big ass up in the air.

"Goddamn, bitch. Hold up, let a nigga breath," Grip spat, trying to catch his breath wondering was this bitch for real.

When he heard the loud knock at the door, he damn near ran out the room. He grabbed his jeans, sans boxer, and headed for the door.

"Who?"

"Open the door."

Grip froze like a mime in Central Park. It was Baby Wise. He looked through the peephole and saw Baby Wise glaring back at him. Grip could make out a shoulder on the side of Baby Wise's, which meant he wasn't alone.

"Shit!" Grip swore under his breath.

Grip rushed back to the bedroom and stepped into his Tims.

"Get dressed."

"Huh?"

"Get dressed, you gotta go!"

She sucked her teeth, but didn't protest, grabbing her sweatpants and t-shirt, because she wore no panties or bra.

Grip threw on a t-shirt inside out, it's only purpose to conceal the .380 he tucked in the small of his back. He didn't think Baby Wise was on to him, but just in case...

His next thought was to call Biz. This was the perfect opportunity to get Baby Wise. He was exposed. But just as quickly as it came to mind was as quickly as he cancelled the thought.

He opened the door and ushered the girl out. As she passed Baby Wise, she eyed him up and down lustfully, but Baby Wise was oblivious to it. His attention was on Grip. He and the three gunners entered the apartment. Grip gave

Baby Wise dap and a gangsta hug.

"What up, son? You caught me with my pants down," Grip joked.

Baby Wise didn't crack a smile.

"You said you wanted to see me, right?" Baby Wise reminded him.

"Yeah, but I ain't know..."

Baby Wise cut him off.

"Times like this, a man should never telegraph his next move, feel me?"

Grip nodded, no doubt.

Baby Wise walked around the room and peeped down the apartment hallway, as if he was inspecting the place.

"This here is crazy right now. The streets is on fire, can't make no money, police everywhere...." Baby Wise shook his head. "We gotta end this shit now."

"Fo sho, my dude."

Baby Wise stepped closer to him, a curious sneer on his face.

"And you know what? I know who set Kane up."

There was no way Grip could go for his gun. He knew he'd never make it. For all he knew, one of Baby Wise's gunners was behind him with a pistol to his head. The thought alone made his knees weak and his throat instantly dry, so when he said, "Who?" it came out as a raspy grunt.

Baby Wise left him in suffering for a moment.

"K.K. and Dick Dick," Baby Wise responded.

Grip felt like he had been playing Russian roulette and the trigger clicked an empty cylinder. The moment when, thinking all is lost to have it all return was like the little death of an orgasm only better. The light returned to Grip's eyes and he grasped onto Baby Wise's words like a drowning man to a branch.

"Word?"

118

Baby Wise nodded, eyeing Grip's reaction closely.

"I called them lil niggas this mornin'. They were supposed to meet me, but I aint heard from 'em since. The shit too simple, I should have seen it sooner, yo. I must be slippin'," Baby Wise remarked.

"That's some foul shit though, but it makes sense. Them, Kane and Smoke together, then only Kane and Smoke get killed? Yeah, shit sounds like a set up," Grip concluded and feeling superior since Baby Wise thought K.K. and Dick Dick did it, it was doubly good that they were already dead. Dead men can't defend themselves against accusations.

"No doubt, good thing you weren't there, huh?" Baby Wise quipped, but Grip failed to catch the sarcasm in his tone.

"Naw Dunn, I wish I woulda been there. Kane might still be here, God bless the dead," Grip replied with all the sincerity his treacherous heart could muster.

"Yeah but..." Baby Wise sighed, "It is what it is. Right now, I need you fam. Can I trust you?"

"No question my nigga. You already know."

"You sure 'cause this is serious, but on the strength of Kane, I know it'll work."

"I'm wit you," Grip answered him.

"I need you to holla at Bacardi. Tell him you think I'm in over my head on this shit, play to his ego. I want you to make him think you willing to set me up for him," Baby Wise explained.

Grip couldn't believe his luck! Baby Wise was giving him the go ahead to do what he was already doing only now he wouldn't have to hide. He could scheme out in the open and right under Baby Wise's nose! He was laughing at Baby Wise's dumb ass, but his face didn't give him away.

"Can you handle that?" Baby Wise quizzed.

"Come on Baby Wise, you know how we do, kid," Grip replied jovially then gave Baby Wise a gangsta hug.

Baby Wise winked at his gunners over Grip's shoulder then said, "I'ma give you Bacardi number. Go hard yo, shit on my name, do whatever it takes to get in with home boy. Just get the drop on the nigga and we'll come through and handle the rest."

Grip nodded. He didn't need Bacardi number because he already had it. Bacardi was obviously keeping him at arm's length, because the only one he met face to face was Biz. But that was cool because Bacardi was safe; it was Baby Wise that had to worry.

"I got you, son. Say no more," Grip answered.

"Then that's what it is then. Let's get this shit over with, then afterwards, D.R. on me, nigga," Baby Wise chuckled.

Baby Wise and his gunners walked out and both men left each other thinking they had the upper hand.

11:07 AM
HALLOWEEN

Déjà vu.......

Everything was about to end as it began...at least for Bop and Mellow. Bop may've been the best driver in Brooklyn, but he was no match for the NYPD when they brought out the big guns. Police choppers, a fleet of police cruisers and the top notch communications system that can't be eluded once the dragnet had been cast. It hadn't been hard to find them either. Once the mayor heard the news about the possibility of the MPV recovered at the East New York crime scene being the same MPV involved in the so-called dirty cop homicide, he went into action. He leaned on the police chief who, in turn, leaned on the detectives in charge of the case. They, in turn, leaned on their informants who knew the four man crew personally.

"Drive the mother fucka nigga!" Mellow barked, as Bop took the corner damn near on the wheels.

"Fuck you think I'm doing?!" He based back.

They both knew there was little chance of getting away, but they had different views of getting caught.

The police cruiser right on their ass bumped the back of the Escalade hard, causing Bop and Mellow to jerk violently in their seats.

"Nigga bust! Get that nigga off my ass!" Bop told Mellow. Mellow reluctantly leaned out the window and purposely shot over the police car. He wasn't trying to shoot a cop. The tactic worked, though, and the officer fell back.

The beating rotor of the chopper over head was so loud in their ears, it sounded like it was right above their heads. Mellow leaned forward and looked up.

"Yo son, it's over! We can't beat 'em! Just pull over!"

Bop looked at him like he had lost his mind. When he saw the look in Mellow's eyes, it turned his stomach. You never know what a man is truly made of until his back is against the wall. What Bop saw was that Mellow was made of jello. Bop knew right then what Mellow would do if they got caught and the thought made him want to kill him on the spot.

"Ride or die, nigga!" Bop hissed, the dust in his system making him feel invincible.

Bop barreled the Escalade through the intersection like a running back, narrowly missing the tail end of a bus, but front ending a Toyota Corolla and knocking it sideways. As he floored the accelerator, he jumped the curb on the next block and cut diagonally through a supermarket parking lot, dodging people, shopping carts and cars.

"Nigga, watch out!"

"I see it!"

Up ahead, spanning Atlantic Avenue was a well-fortified roadblock, two lines of cruisers with officers behind cars and open doors, their weapons aimed and ready. Bop slammed on the brakes and the entire police force let loose a barrage of gun fire that sparked the Escalade and blew out the front left tire.

"Damn!" Bop huffed, driving in reverse as another cruiser came up and slammed into the back of the SUV.

Amped and death struck, Bop jumped from the car,

and spun on the cruiser, firing recklessly. One shot went through the driver's neck and exploded out the headrest. The firepower that the police unleashed cut Bop to shreds, spinning him like a top. As blood spurted from his body at all angles, Bop laughed in the face of the rage until he hit the ground lifeless.

Meanwhile, Mellow was paralyzed, surrounded by police, and seeing his man gunned down in a hysterical rage had drained the fight from his spirit.

"Don't fuckin' move!"

"Get out of the car and down on the ground!"

Mellow complied with the quickness and was swarmed in a sea of blue.

"So what you got to say tough guy?"

"I ain't got shit to say. I want my lawyer."

"You want a lawyer? Here's your lawyer!"

Blah!

The linebacker-sized Detective Morelli smacked Mellow so hard, he flipped backwards out of his chair and landed awkwardly and painfully because his hands were cuffed tightly behind his back.

Morelli snatched him off the ground and slammed him against the cinder block wall of the interrogation room.

"That's the kind of lawyer cop killers get!" Morelli barked in his face.

"Cop killer?! I ain't no fuckin' cop killer! You got the wrong one, that ain't me."

"Yeah?" Morelli sneered menacingly. "I coulda sworn that was you who killed Officer Burns, didn't you Joe?"

The slimmer Polish detective smoked his cigarette, tipped back in his chair on two legs.

"Yep.... That's what I saw, too," said Wakowski.

"You a goddamn lie!" Mellow hissed.

123

Wakowski snickered.

"Maybe a little white lie, but it's the kind juries believe."

Morelli sat Mellow's chair back up then slammed him back in it. He sat on the edge of the desk.

"What? You thought that dead, cock-sucker of a friend of yours is gonna get off that easy? He killed a cop and somebody's gonna wear it! So, I figure why not you? Unless," Morelli let his voice trail off.

"Unless what?" Mellow growled.

"You tell us about the robbery in Queens. How'd you get a hold of a cop car?" Wakowski probed.

"I don't know nothing about no robbery and like I said, get me a fucking lawyer!" Mellow bellowed.

Morelli got off the desk so fast; Mellow flinched, thinking he was going to hit him again. Morelli smiled at his fear. He got up close to his ear and said softly, "See, when a cop is killed, the rules change. All's fair, you follow me? We get vindictive, conniving...fucking ruthless, and you don't want that, right? You want a lawyer? Fine it's your life and you can kiss your ass good-bye. Cause if we walk outta here, then fuck that robbery, its murder one of a police officer. And we got ways of making it stick. You fuckin' clear?"

Morelli straightened up and eyed Mellow. After a brief silence, Mellow looked up at Morelli standing over top of him.

"What you wanna know?"

Morelli smiled at Wakowski.

11:45 A.M.
HALLOWEEN

"These are Renee Owen's phone records," Detective Little said as he handed the printout to Natasha.

She and Rahjohn were at sitting at their desks positioned side by side. Rahjohn was on the phone, as she hung up hers and looked up at Detective Little.

"Thanks," Natasha replied, looking at the sheets. "What's these?" she started to ask, but Little cut her off.

"I took the liberty of highlighting any recurring numbers, red for most frequent, yellow for less frequent and blue for hear and there repeats."

"I'm assuming the numbers without addresses are prepaid numbers," Natasha remarked.

"Yep, which as you can see are mostly the red highlights."

Natasha sighed.

"And whoever she was talking to not long before she was murdered was prepaid, too. No chance of getting a copy of her text messages for that day?"

Little shook his head.

"Not without a court order."

"Make it happen," she told him.

"I'm on it," he replied, walking away.

Rahjohn hung up and ran his hand over his waves.

"Well, just in case you're taking score, add two more to Bacardi's column."

"Another shooting?"

"On Guy Brewer. They confirmed them from the surveillance cams at J. Malone's party. They were the two shooters that got away," Rahjohn explained.

Natasha handed him the phone records.

"Renee Owen's phone records," she said then adding, "It's not much to go on except the address of 114-22 139th, the only number that is repeated over and over and is not prepaid."

"And she talked to..." he scanned the page for a name, "Kenneth Carey for twenty minutes before she was killed. It's worth a shot," Rahjohn proposed.

The phone rang on Rahjohn's desk.

Homicide Detective Griffin." His eyes lit up and he gave Natasha the thumbs up sign. "In Brooklyn? Okay, that's great, Chief. Is he talking? Okay. I'm on it."

Rahjohn hung up and looked at Natasha.

"They just collared a guy in Brooklyn that they believe ran with the victims in the East New York shootings," Rahjohn told her as he stood up, grabbing his coat off the back of the chair.

Natasha stood with him.

"What case? Morelli and Wakowski?" Natasha asked.

"Unfortunately."

"Ass holes."

"Hey, Griffin," Detective Little called from across the room. "Detective Morelli from Brooklyn on line one."

"Speaking of the devil," Rahjohn smirked holding a finger in the air, as he headed back to his desk and picked up the phone.

"Griffin. Yeah, we heard. Is that right? Maybe we will

solve this thing after all. We're on our way."

Rahjohn hung up then walked toward Natasha.

"Guess who wants to talk now? Rahjohn smirked.

"No," Natasha replied, already sensing the answer. "You think she knows about the collar?"

Rahjohn shrugged.

"We'll find out soon enough."

As they exited the building, Rahjohn's cell phone rang. Even without answering he knew who it was with one glance at his watch.

"You're late. It's 12:05," Rahjohn remarked sarcastically.

Autumn smiled at Bacardi.

"So does that mean you don't want to see me?"

"What do you think? Where you wanna meet?"

"Far Rockaway, you know the New Haven Plaza?" The movie Unknown is playing, meet me there. Bacardi'll never think I'm in Far Rockaway," she snickered, winking at Bacardi. He sipped his drink and winked back.

"I'm on my way, Rahjohn replied.

"I'm sure you are, Detective."

Autumn hung up.

"It's all good?" Bacardi inquired.

"You already know."

She sat back, wrapping her arms playfully around his neck.

Bacardi patted her ass.

"Ma, get in that nigga head, word. Find..."

Autumn put her finger to his lips then kissed him softly.

"I know my position. Now watch me play it."

Rahjohn ended the conversation as he and Natasha reached the car. He handed her the keys.

"Tash, that was Bacardi's chick. I almost forgot I was supposed to meet her," he lied. Actually, he was looking forward to it and filled with the anticipation. He was purposely trying to find a way to meet her. Now, it seemed that luck was on his side.

"Couldn't have worked out better if you planned it yourself," she quipped, opening the car door.

Rahjohn ignored her sarcasm.

"Soon as I'm done, I'll meet you in Brooklyn, the 111th."

"Goodbye, Rahjohn," Natasha replied, getting in and starting the car.

He smiled playfully.

"No kiss?"

"I got something for you to kiss, alright, close my door," she spat back, then shut the door herself with a thud.

Why do I even let him get me upset? she thought to herself.

"I'll call you," Rahjohn told her, heading to his personal car.

Antoinette lay on her side with her back to the cop, pretending to be sleep. In reality, she was texting.

The nurse Autumn had spoken to was five hundred dollars richer for simply running out and buying a twenty dollar phone and minute card, then slipping it to Antoinette when she brought her lunch tray.

I'm hit! Murder 1! King's County Hospital! Make it Happen!

Vita texted back, almost instantly.

I know. We already on it. 1

Vita put down the phone and looked into the bathroom, hearing the sizzle of the shower water. She was glad Antoinette was alright. But now she was being held on murder one, two counts. The only good thing was she was being held in the hospital for now. That wouldn't last for long, so she knew she had to get out and make some things happen. But first she had to get past Baby Wise.

Vita took her oversized t-shirt off as she headed for the bathroom. Underneath, was her deliciously chocolate 36-23-38 edible proportioned frame. She caught a vision of herself in the mirror as she walked back and gave herself a wink and an air kiss.

Baby Wise was in the shower, allowing the sizzling hot water to cascade down his entire body. Baby Wise loved when the water steamed the whole room and damn near scalded his body. The sensation helped to relax him and helped clear his mind. The events of the last twelve hours played back in his head like a bootleg hood flick. Somebody had once said, 'life was a game with a lot of rules but no referee'. No wonder so many people choose to cheat.

He shook his head at the lack of loyalty, and solidness in the game today. It was at the point where nothing anybody did surprised him anymore, not even Bacardi or Grip.

Grip.

The name alone tasted like shit in Baby Wise's mouth, that ungrateful son of a bitch. He and Kane had put him on when he was flat broke and pissy, and this was how he chose to repay? But then again, it's always the one you feed because no matter how much you give them, it's never enough.

Baby Wise had been the call in Grip's pocket that had set the whole chain of events that proved his disloyalty. Phones are so sensitive nowadays that all it takes is the slightest touch to answer them. During Grip's struggle with K.K., he had done just that. Baby Wise played the message on his phone over and over. He heard the muffled voices and the gunshots. The last thing he heard was Dick-Dick.

"Yous a snake ass nigga, Grip!"

He recognized Dick-Dick's voice clearly. Then he heard the final shot and that's how he knew and it all made sense. Baby Wise was always one step ahead. He saw the opportunity in Grips treachery and he didn't hesitate to utilize it. That's why he went to Grip, containing his anger and rage and gave Grip his mission. Baby Wise figured if Grip had switched sides, then he could lead Baby Wise right to Bacardi. Therefore, Baby Wise had his people sit outside Grip's apartment building, to follow him. And when he met up with Bacardi....

Baby Wise's thoughts were interrupted when he felt Vita's hand gripping his dick as she slipped into the shower behind him.

"You gonna use up all the hot water by yourself?" she purred seductively.

Baby Wise smiled.

"What? You want some?"

"No daddy, I want it all," she whispered, turning Baby Wise toward her and sitting of the edge of the tub.

She took his dick in her hand gently stroking him before she put him in her mouth.

"Well, good mornin' to you too," she giggled, kissing the head of his dick several times before she licked down his shaft and sucked his balls, one by one.

Baby Wise leaned against the wall with a grunt, keeping eye contact with Vita as she curled his toes with her oral expertise.

"You like that baby?"

"You already know; if the head right, Biggie there every night."

With that, Vita devoured his hard long manhood, engulfing him with her lust. Even though she had an ulterior motive, Vita loved to suck dick. She loved the power and control that it gave her over a man's pleasure and in another way, his mind. She vigorously stroked her hand up and down the shaft, while running her tongue in the tiny hole at the tip of his dick. Then she massaged it with the depth of her throat, putting her hand on his ass and urging him to fuck her face.

"Yeah? You want daddy to dick your mouth like a pussy?"

Vita's eyes answered affirmatively.

"Eat that dick," then he grunted, grabbing both sides of her head and began dicking her mouth.

He was pumping her so fast, from time to time, he could hear a slight gag in back of her throat which turned Baby Wise on and made him dick her harder.

"Ugghh, yeah baby, swallow it all for daddy," Baby Wise grumbled, leaning against the wall as he bent over, his hands holding her face as his body jerked with the last of his load which of course Vita swallowed.

Vita could tell by the look on his face that she had him right where she wanted him.

"Daddy," she said still milking his dick, licking the clear, post-cum. "I need a favor."

12:11 P.M.
HALLOWEEN

Grip pulled his Benz in the C-Town parking lot in Hollis. "I'm here," he said to Biz over the phone.

"I see you," Biz replied.

Grip saw a black Nissan Altima pull out and pull up, driver's door to driver's door with Grip's Benz. Inside was Biz and two of his goons.

"So, what was so important you needed to see me again? I told you, handle your B.I. then get at me," Biz stated firmly, his distrust apparent from the way he kept scanning the parking lot. His two goons got out and held vigil.

"Naw Dunn, this shit is so fuckin' sweet," Grip smirked, arrogant in his ignorance of Baby Wise's true intentions.

"The nigga came to see me, and peep it, he wants me to get at you and set you up!" He laughed.

"Who, Baby Wise? He came to see you? Why you ain't call like you was supposed to?" Biz hissed, gripping the gun in his lap.

Grip heard the intensity in Biz's voice and quickly tried to placate it.

"Just chill, Dunn. It ain't even like that. The nigga didn't call or nothin'. He just showed up."

"Maybe he don't trust you and he didn't want you to know he was comin'," Biz suggested. "You ever thought of that?"

Grip laughed arrogantly.

"Get the fuck outta here. Of course he trusts me, Dunn. If he even thought I couldn't be trusted, I'd be dead," Grip admitted, thinking back to the anxiety he felt in Baby Wise's presence.

Biz nodded, visibly relaxing.

"True indeed," he said, thinking for a minute then he smiled. "Shit is a slick move though. Glad we thought of it first."

The two uneasy allies shared their first and last laugh together.

"Ai-ight yo, let me holla, at Bacardi, see how he wanna handle this and I'ma get at you."

"One."

"One," Biz replied, then leaned out the car window and said to his goons, "Let's go."

They pulled off in opposite directions. Biz tried Antoinette for the umpteenth time, again getting her voice mail but it was full. He angrily texted her:

Where the fuck you at!

He pocketed his phone. It wasn't like Antoinette not to call him or to turn off her phone. *Maybe her battery is dead or maybe something happened to her. Maybe Baby Wise....*

He shook the thought out of his head and the worry out of his heart. He had to keep focused. He was balls deep in war.

"I'm telling you yo, this bitch is a freak. I had her like this, Dunn...." Biz heard one of his goons say to the other. As he drove, he kept his eyes open and it was a good thing that he did.

He didn't recognize it at first, but after making three Turns, he still saw the blue Cobalt tailing behind him. He recognized it for what it was.

"Bitch ass nigga tried to set us up!" Biz growled. His man in the passenger seat started to turn around, but Biz stopped him. "Naw, just chill, don't look."

The only sounds in the car were the metallic ratchets of cocking automatic weapons.

"What up, Dunn? How we gonna do this?" his man in the back seat asked.

"I told Bacardi this nigga was a snake! If he crossed his man that easy, why the fuck wouldn't he cross us? Fuck that, we gettin' this nigga," he hissed, pulling out his phone and hitting speed dial.

"Yep."

"A blue Chevy.... Looks like a Cobalt, yeah a Cobalt. Got it? A Cobalt."

"Yeah, yeah, a Cobalt. What up?"

You already know what it is!"

"Say no more."

Click.

Baby Wise's team, seven niggas deep, had followed Grip to the C-Town meeting with Biz. They had called Baby Wise twice, but didn't get an answer. The third time he picked up. But, by that time, Biz was pulling off.

"Follow him," Baby Wise told them when they explained the situation, and they did just that.

The first few blocks they managed to conceal themselves in traffic, but as traffic thinned out, it became harder to keep out of sight. They weren't experienced enough to give Biz a block, alternating speeds to tail and fade. Therefore, Biz was on to them, a fact one of Baby Wise's team expressed.

"I'm telling you man, he sees us," the passenger of the blue Cobalt said.

"Naw yo, we good," the driver replied, but even he had doubts.

"Fuck this creep shit. Floor this shit and rock that nigga to sleep," one of the dudes in the back seat suggested aggressively.

"Baby Wise said follow 'em!"

"Fuck that, call Baby Wise."

And they did. Baby Wise, instantly grasping the situation knew the chances of Biz not seeing them were slim. So, he saw no other choice.

"Fuck it then, handle 'em," Baby Wise instructed.

They understood exactly what he meant.

They picked the next light as the ambush point and tried to pull up beside Biz to gun him down. But Biz was already aware of their presence and anticipated their next move.

"Here they come!" Biz said, adrenaline percolating in his blood like hot java.

He purposely gave himself enough distance from the car ahead of him to not get boxed in, making it easy for him to dip into the empty on-coming lane at the light, and make a wide right merging quickly with the intersecting traffic.

That's when he heard the first shots pierce the trunk of his car.

"I told you he was on point!" the passenger based, his Heckler and Koch 416 barking shots out the window.

He still ain't getting away though!" the driver of the Cobalt vowed, expertly mimicking Biz's maneuver and getting in behind him. The Cobalt was in the left lane, the Altima in the right, a little more than a car length apart, and shots were now being exchanged with murderous intensity as the cars sped down the street. Windows were shattered, and both car bodies looked like Swiss cheese, until one accurate shot from the goon in the back seat of the Cobalt picked Biz off, hitting him in the left shoulder.

"Fuck, I'm hit! Get them niggas, I'm hit," Biz agonized, fighting to keep control of the car.

He made a hard left against traffic, buying a little time because the Cobalt had to swerve and fish tail to keep from avoiding a head on collision, then the driver of the Cobalt floored the gas pedal again in pursuit of Biz.

Biz made a tire-squealing right onto his block where the ambush awaited. The block appeared empty as they gunned down on Biz's bumper just as a black van parked on the side of the street swerved out into the street and rammed the side of the Cobalt hard, pushing it into a row of parked cars on the opposite side of the street.

Sparks flew as the Cobalt skidded along the length of a Cadillac before rear ending a Suburban, throwing driver and passenger into a face full of air bags.

Tssssssss! Boom! The air bags inflated, cushioning the impact, but nothing could cushion the impact of the barrage of bullets that filled the car. Still dazed from the accident, the occupants of the Cobalt didn't get off another shot. Biz's ambush team surrounded the Cobalt and proceeded to execute all four men mercilessly with AK-47s that literally blew them to pieces.

Biz staggered from the Altima, his whole shirt red from blood gushing from his shoulder.

"Yo, get me to Doc's," he told one of his goons who quickly escorted him to another car and skirted off.

2:27 P.M.
HALLOWEEN

Rahjohn stopped at the door, letting his eyes adjust to the darkness of the theatre. The scene on the screen was a night scene, which didn't help his attempt to scan the pitch black rows of seats. Fortunately, there weren't too many patrons and the theatre was practically empty. When the screen lit up with a bust of color, Rahjohn was able to spot Autumn on the far right side of the theatre.

He made his way over and slid into the seat next to her. She offered him some popcorn. He declined.

"It took a minute to spot you. You could've waved or something," he remarked, studying her profile, confirming what he already knew. She was the prettiest woman he had ever laid eyes on.

Autumn shrugged, putting a few kernels in her mouth.

"Why? I thought you said you could find me."

He didn't respond. He just smiled and looked at the screen, amused with how nonchalantly she had reminded him of his own words that he said to her at the hospital.

"I didn't know you were into vampire flicks."

"I'm not. So it'll be the last place anybody would think

137

I'd be," she replied. "Besides, it's not a vampire flick."

"Naw?"

"It's a love story."

"Oh, so the guy gets the girl?"

"Not in this one."

"Then it'll be a sequel, huh?" Rahjohn quipped and made Autumn giggle. The sound of her voice made him want to find ways to make her giggle again, but he reminded himself....

Stay focused.

"Your boyfriend's run is about to come to an end, you know that right?"

"My man... has been through worse," she countered, looking at the screen.

For some reason, the fact that she emphasized man in her reply bothered Rahjohn, but he didn't know why.

Stay focused.

"Still willing to take your chances, I see," he retorted, looking at her silhouette and the way the soft colors from the screen illuminated her features.

Autumn fixed him with a serious look.

"That's what people do when they don't have choices. They take chances."

"You always have a choice."

She smiled condescendingly, like one does in the face of naivety.

"Where are you from, Detective Griffin?"

"Rahjohn."

"Okay, Rahjohn."

"Harlem. Why?"

"Oh, I see, home of the pretty boys and hustlers. You've got the pretty part down pat, you just don't understand the hustle," she remarked. It was as if she was challenging his hood card, something no man born and raised in the ghetto liked, cop or no cop.

"Oh, I understand it, alright. My father was a hustler,

and so were my uncles, the ones that ain't dead or in jail."

"Your father?"

"Dead," he replied, turning to look at the screen. "So I understand it's a no win situation. I learned from their examples."

She let that marinate for a moment, then said, "I'm from Queensbridge. And the Bridge is like a world of its own. You could spend your whole life in the Bridge and never know anything else existed. Shit, I didn't until I was nine. Guess where I went?"

He looked at her for the answer.

"Coney Island," she giggled. "But you know what I did know? I knew we were poor. Me, my mama, my four sisters and my grandma, we had nothing coming up. Three generations all lived inside the Bridge and not a damn thing to show for it."

Rahjohn could hear the bitterness in her voice. He wanted to say something to soothe her, but he wasn't there to soothe, he was there for answers....

Stay focused.

"I've always been pretty. You know what it's like being pretty in the hood? Well, a pretty girl in the hood," she smiled and briefly touched his hand. The sensation of her skin on his didn't go unnoticed. She shook her head, "All the women want to fight you and all the men want to fuck you...even when you're ...."

Her voice trailed off and he knew exactly what it was that she didn't say. He despised child molesters, and to hear that someone had done that to Autumn made him boil inside.

"Ay yo, a nigga like that..."

"Brought me into this world," she snapped, and the coldness in her eyes and the reality in her statement hit him like a Tyson punch. Rahjohn dropped his head.

"I'm not here to use you," Rahjohn stated sincerely,

looking her in the eyes. "But this thing with Bacardi and Baby Wise is out of hand. And if you're not careful, it could be your body I'm standing over."

"Then you are trying to use me, Rahjohn," she snickered, but before he could protest, she added, "But that's what makes the world go round. I'm a big girl, baby. I understand the cards you dealin'. You want Bacardi and you want me to help you or talk enough until you can help yourself."

"Or help you," he stated, looking in her eyes.

"Just like that, huh?" she nodded at the screen. "Just like in the movies," she said sarcastically.

He inclined toward her and replied, "Look, I know you don't know me. And I know you're not about to trust me, hell you probably don't even like cops, I'm sure you probably hate cops. And that's okay. I can deal with that. And yeah, I want your man, I want him bad. But I won't use you to get him. All I'm offering is an opportunity, and that window's steadily closing. Because once the boat sinks, not even I can save you."

Autumn looked at him evenly, studying his face. Her eyes caressed the contours of his face, from his razor sharp edge up, his smooth cocoa complexion and thick, bushy eyebrows to his suckable lips. Then she looked straight into his brown eyes.

"Why? Why you wanna save me?" she asked intently.

The softness of her voice, the tinge of vulnerability in her tone and the search in her eyes was reason alone to bring out the protector in him, so he had to remind himself again...

Stay focused.

"Because you wouldn't have come if you didn't want to be."

The question on Autumn's face converted into a smile. After a moment, she turned back to the screen.

140

"You know he sent me here," she told him.

"Who?"

"Who you think?"

He nodded.

"He wants me to get in your head and see what you know," she admitted.

Rahjohn's heart seemed to drop to his stomach.

"So that's why you came?"

She eyed him with a mischievous grin.

"No, but it was a perfect excuse, huh?"

Stay focused....

Antoinette moved slowly, like an old woman, holding on to her iron walking wheels. She pushed herself toward the bathroom. The female cop sitting in the chair reading an Ebony Magazine looked up grilling her.

"Bathroom... goddamn," Antoinette huffed, tired of her every move being watched. The only place she had any privacy was in the hospital bathroom, and privacy is what she desperately needed at the moment.

She pulled the small flat cell phone out and dialed Bacardi's number.

No answer.

Thinking the reason he didn't answer was because he didn't recognize the number, she texted him. A few minutes later she called and he answered, just as she flushed the toilet.

"Yo."

"Bacardi," she said whispering his name.

"I can't hear you. What's that noise?"

"The toilet," she replied. "Your girl Autumn came to holla at me."

"I know ma, I sent her. We wanted to make sure you was good," he lied, smooth as brandy. "You talk to Biz yet?"

She sucked her teeth and flushed the toilet.

"He the reason I'm in here."

"Huh? I can't hear you. What, you shittin'?"

"No boy," she snickered. "The police right outside the door."

"Oh, now what you say?"

"I said Biz is the reason I'm here."

Bacardi's ears perked up.

"What you mean by that?"

Silence.

"Yo nette, talk to me, ma," he urged her.

She flushed the toilet. "I... I swear, I didn't want to do it, Bacardi. Please don't do nothin' to me," she whined, smiling to herself.

Bacardi sensed that she was about to pull his coat, which made him proceed with caution. Besides, she was in police custody. If she felt threatened, who knew what she might say or do? And she could easily be cooperating with them in exchange for protection.

"Listen, ma, you ain't got nothin' to worry about. A woman 'posed to ride for her man. You just ridin' for the wrong nigga, that's all," he crooned as convincingly as he could.

Antoinette recognized the irony. They were both trying to fool the other.

"You just saying that, Bacardi. You don't even know the half."

"Look, Antoinette, I know you go hard and I know you a loyal chick. I could see myself fuckin' wit you hard body, but this is your only chance. Did Biz have something to do wit' this shit?"

"Yes," she whispered timidly. "He...he set the whole thing up?" she lied then proceeded to explain how Biz had pulled it off. The icing on the cake was when she sat there out her mouth and said, "And then, he put the bag in the hallway closet, behind the vacuum cleaner box."

Bacardi had heard all he needed to hear. She had just signed Biz's death warrant. He wasn't even mad now that he knew. He just knew that he had to handle that. It was just business.

"Okay, listen Antoinette, it's all good, okay? My beef ain't wit' you. The sniffle he heard in her voice seemed so real, so distraught. If only he could see the smile on her face.

"No... no, I kept my mouth shut. But they got me for murder and..."

"I already know, and my word; I'ma handle it. I'ma get you the best lawyer and we'll beat this. I know you a down broad. I got you," he promised truthfully.

There was no way he'd leave her hanging. She was already pissed at Biz. If she decides to flip on Biz, Bacardi had no doubt she'd flip on him too. Therefore, since he couldn't kill her, the next best thing was to take care of her for now.

"Okay Bacardi, I'ma hold it down, okay?"

"Indeed, that's a good girl. Now fall back. Can I hit you at this number?"

"Text me first."

"Be easy, sweetness. I got you."

Click.

"No sweetness, I got you."

She opened the door to find Natasha waiting for her.

"So this was a war just waiting to happen, huh?" Rahjohn asked. Rahjohn and Autumn were sitting on the plush white leather sectional in the Far Rockaway apartment Autumn called 'Bacardi's Bank of New York'. She opened a bottle of vitamin water, sipped, then sat down next to him.

"Ex-actly, all it needed was the right spark. Baby

Wise and Bacardi were already on shaky ground because of the Hollis - Southside thing, but they got over it for the sake of money. But, on the low, Baby Wise was jealous of Bacardi. Biz knew all that, and believe me, Biz was always a grimy dude."

"So, you think Biz set this up?" he asked, thinking about everything she had told him.

"Probably, but what I think doesn't matter to hear Bacardi tell it.

"So, he sent you to the hospital to see what Antoinette knew?"

"Exactly."

"Or whether or not she told the police anything."

"Did she?" Autumn smirked, eyeing Rahjohn as she sipped her vitamin water.

"Rahjohn acted like he didn't hear her. Instead, he asked, "So, what about Renee Owens?"

"What about her."

"Could Biz have used her to help set everything up?"

"Biz wouldn't have needed Renee for nothing. He handled the deal, so it woulda been easy to turn it into a setup," Autumn explained.

"So why is she dead? She had to know something."

"Believe me, Renee would've never agreed to help set Bacardi up."

"Because he was payin' her?"

"Because he was fuckin' her," Autumn smirked. "Don't look so surprised."

"You knew?" Rahjohn asked, mildly surprised.

"Of course I did," she shrugged. "I know about a lot of chicks, including the one that's pregnant by him now. But as long as he takes care of home, you get used to things like that."

"The glamorous life of a hustler's wife, huh?" he quipped with a tinge of resentment in his voice,

144

Autumn laughed.

"Stop playin', it ain't just hustlers. All men do it, that is, at least the cats worth having. The ones that ain't broke, gay, pussy whipped or cripple. You can't tell me you don't cheat on your girl," Autumn challenged.

"Naw, baby, I don't have a girlfriend," he shot back smoothly.

"Ohh, then you have many girlfriends," she laughed and he couldn't help but to join her. "Yeah," she continued, "I shoulda known. Fine as you are, smooth as you move and you come with hand cuffs! I bet the chicks can't keep their hands off of you," she purred, caressing his cheek with her thumb.

Stay...focused.

Antoinette took her time answering, deciding not to as she fumbled with the TV remote connected to her hospital bed. She fluffed the pillow behind her back, until she was comfortable. The whole time, Natasha remained patiently quiet and observant. She didn't like Antoinette, so she was determined not to let her get under her skin.

"So," Antoinette began, pushing the button to make the bed sit up a little more, "Where's that fine boyfriend of yours?" she asked with a goofy grin.

Natasha just looked at her without responding.

"Oh, I forgot, you're on the job, so he's your..." she raised her index and ring fingers to make the quotation gesture, "partner, right?" she shook her head already knowing the deal. "But between you and me, I know ya'll fuckin'. Shit, fine as he is, I'd be fuckin' him, too."

"Look, you wanna talk or play games," Natasha asked firmly.

"Both, let's talk about playing games," Antoinette cracked. "This is Halloween, right? But instead of putting them on, I'm about to take all the masks off," Antoinette winked.

Rahjohn leaned his face away from Autumn's caress, reluctantly but decisive, trying to stay focused.

"So, if she wasn't killed to cover the set up, why do you think she was killed," he questioned.

"I don't know. But tell me something, are you always a cop," she quizzed, biting down on her bottom lip slightly. "What I mean is, when you first saw me, what was the first thing that came to your mind?"

That you are the baddest chick I've ever seen in my life and it's all going to waste on a no good motherfucker like Bacardi, he thought, but he lied with a shrug. "I don't remember."

The sensual giggle she gave played up and down his spine like piano keys.

"I thought cops were good liars. I remember the first thing I thought. It was your eyebrows, so thick and bushy. I had this crazy urge to smooth them for you. Can I?"

Stay... focused.

"You trust him?"

"Trust who?"

"Your boyfriend?"

Natasha glanced up from taking notes, her poker face in place.

"Let's just stick to the subject, okay. So, you're telling me that your boyfriend set this whole thing up?"

"That's what I said, aint it? And why you can't answer my questions?" Antoinette replied.

Natasha sighed hard, but in order to get it over with, she played Hannibal Lector and answered her, "Yes, I trust him!"

Antoinette started laughing at Natasha and for some strange reason she couldn't stop.

"You hear this fool? Don't she know, the words trust and him don't go in the same sentence?! Wow, where they do that at?"

Antoinette's laughter started to get under Natasha's skin. She stood there expressionless looking at Antoinette as she rolled around in her hospital bed unable to control her self. *Just keep it together, don't let her get to you.*

"He's just my partner, but trust me; it's not what you think it is!" Natasha responded defensively.

"No, trust me; it's exactly what I think it is."

Then she started humming a tune. "It's written all over your face," Antoinette sang, before she busted back out in a burst of her own laughter.

This bitch is crazy. If we weren't in this hospital right now I'd punch her in her face as hard as I could. Natasha imagined knocking the shit out of Antoinette. A slight smile spread across her face. And even though Natasha didn't want to admit it, Antoinette had gotten to her, so she snapped back.

"And you know what's written all over your face? Guilty, two counts of murder one! That's what you need to worry about, because if we don't have your full cooperation then you'll never see the light of day!"

Antoinette smirked with her lips twisted. *That's right bitch I see you getting emotional. You ain't even gonna have time to think and you ain't never gonna see it coming,* she thought amusedly.

"He told you to do this, too?" Rahjohn grunted, firmly gripping her wrist just short of his eyebrow.

Autumn slid over closer to him.

"No," she replied, "and if he knew that I was, he'd have us both killed."

The sincerity in her reply, and the hunger in her eyes, told Rahjohn that this is all her doing, so against his better judgment, his professional ethics and police decorum, he leaned in to meet her kiss.

The first kiss was a spark that ignited a lustful hunger from within. The second kiss was sloppy, wet and animalistic. They groped at one another, tearing away articles of clothing like excited little kids opening gifts on Christmas day.

"Ahh, I wanted to do this the moment I laid eyes on you," she groaned with so much passion in her voice, it trembled.

"Me too," he agreed, pulling her skirt over her head.

"Baby wait, come to the bedroom," she purred with a playful giggle, backing away from him in the hall.

Rahjohn pinned her to the wall, pulling her bra straps off her shoulders and down around her waist. He sucked and nibbled on her hard brown nipples as he lifted her off her feet and feasted on her flesh. The sensation had her panties so wet she was ready to cum.

"But you still haven't told me who was the female in the Crown Vic," Natasha reminded her, interrupting Antoinette's story.

And you still haven't given me any guarantees on my deal," Antoinette shot right back.

Natasha sighed hard.

Look, I can assure you we'll do everything we can."

"Bullshit," Antoinette huffed defiantly, "Ain't shit ya'll can do to protect me from Bacardi or Baby Wise's people in Rikers or any jail in New York for that matter!"

"Nothing's going to happen to you," Natasha repeated

confidently.

"Look," Antoinette said, sitting up straighter not playing no games. "What I'm about to tell you, you gonna make sergeant, because of it. This case is gonna make your career, feel me? You think this is just a robbery?" Antoinette laughed. "You don't know the half of it. But, you gotta pay to play, and the price for information is I don't see the inside of no jail. You give me that and I guarantee you it'll be worth your while."

Natasha's ambition made her contemplate Antoinette's words.

Not everybody knows how to fuck on a waterbed but for Rahjohn, it was pure sexual physics. The slightest motion created the opposite effect. You press down, it swells up, you move left, it bubbles right, so you can't stroke against the wave, because then it's like having your legs swept out from under you, you lose momentum. You have to ride the wave, synchronizing your rhythm, using the motion to emphasize your thrusts. And that was exactly what Rahjohn was doing as he long dicked Autumn into a passionate frenzy.

Her body was perfect, not one flaw, unbelievable. It had him mesmerized as she lay on her side. He had her body underneath his, missionary, while he drilled her pussy on his knees, tweaking her clit with every stroke.

"Ohhh fuck! That dick feels so goooood," she groaned, her high pinched sexual melody had Rahjohn in a zone.

"Throw it back, harder," Rahjohn growled through clenched teeth.

Autumn's pussy was so wet it was talking to him with wet slurps, stroke for stroke. He began grinding her pussy hard until he slid his thumb in her ass and twisted it slowly.

"B...b...Baby, I can't stop cumin," she gasped as she creamed his dick for the fourth time. Never in her life had she came back to back like that. It only made her horny for more. "Turn me over."

You don't want it from the back, you don't want it. You think you do, but you don't. He couldn't help joking to himself as he thought of tearing her pussy up doggie-style.

Rahjohn slid his long hard rod out long enough for Autumn to assume the face down, ass up position and plunged right back in. The way she was backing it up and matching his aggression, made him fall for the challenge, and he loved it. He gripped her ass cheeks and spread them wide and began to punish her pussy like a madman.

"Ouu-eee, daddy, oh my god, please!" Autumn screamed, burying her face in the pillow to muffle the sounds.

"Take it like a big girl! Take this dick like a big girl!" he growled, biting down aggressively on his bottom lip.

"Yes! Yes! I am!" she moaned in lustful agony, making Rahjohn mash her even harder.

"Cu...cum with me baby, please!"

Several strokes later as Autumn's pussy exploded for the fifth time, Rahjohn came, then collapsed on top of her, exhausted.

"Like I said, I could give em' all to you on a silver platter," Antoinette bragged. "I can break down the whole operation from who's the connect, to where the stash houses are, and all the players involved. This is gonna be the biggest case of your career," Antoinette said full of game.

Natasha smirked.

"Tell me who the female was?"

Antoinette eyed her evenly for a moment then answered, "Not yet, not until we have a deal. But I will say that she is a cop," Antoinette lied.

Natasha nodded, her mind working a thousand miles

a second. It was hard enough for a woman to move up in the ranks of the NYPD, but with a case like this, her name could ring bells at One Police Plaza for years.

"Let me talk to a few people," Natasha said unknowingly.

"Yeah, you do that, 'cause bottom line, I'm staying in this hospital until this thing is cleared up, or I clam up and take my chances on beatin' my case on self-defense. The ball's in your court."

Antoinette was geeking the shit out of Natasha, playing her bluff game to the hilt with no trump card. She knew the police would never let her stay in custody at the hospital. But she needed to buy as much time as she could because she knew, once the plan was complete, it would be nothing for her peoples to waltz her out of there.

Autumn rested her chin on Rahjohn's chest and smiled into his eyes. "You're a good man, Rahjohn. I wish I would've met you ten years ago."

"Well, you met me now," he replied, as if that was all that mattered.

"Do you believe everything happens for a reason?"

He shrugged, "Yeah, I believe there is a method to all the madness in the world. It just takes a better man than me to see it."

Rahjohn recognized that look in her eyes like she wanted to tell him something, just like last night at the club. When she started to speak, he heard her cell ring tone in the living room, and Autumn smiled a tight smile.

"Well," she sighed, "back to reality," she remarked because she knew who it was.

"You know you don't have to go back," he told her.

She traced his lips with her thumb.

"Yeah... I wish that was true."

"Only you can make it true, Autumn. You still have time to walk away." Rahjohn leaned his elbow behind her and brushed her hair out of her face. "Like I just said, only you can make it true, ma," he said softly.

Autumn shook her head solemnly.

"I wish it was that simple, Rahjohn, but it's not. Bacardi would never just let me go. He calls me his 'biggest investment'," she commented bitterly, "All the clothes, the jewelry, the cars and besides, I know too much. He's not letting me go."

Rahjohn sat up near her.

"Bullshit! You ain't his slave."

Her phone rings again.

"I'd better answer that," she whispered, as she hurried out of the room.

Rahjohn collected his clothes, a shoe here, and a sock there that were strewn from bedroom to living room. He was heated, and the more he heard Autumn talk to Bacardi on the phone, the hotter he got.

"I was in the bedroom, Sean, okay?" Autumn lied, looking up as Rahjohn came into the room, stepping into his pants.

She looked so delicious standing there, one arm folded under her breast and her weight on her right foot.

"I left him at the movies. I'll tell you when I get back," she said, tossing Rahjohn his shirt from the couch.

"Okay, okay... As soon as I leave the salon... of course, Sean, I'm safe...okay... me too," she said as she hung up, and Rahjohn knew Bacardi had said, 'I love you', when she replied 'me too'. It was one of the lines he used on chicks.

"We gotta go," she said, heading past him, back into the bedroom. Rahjohn, fully dressed, leaned against the bedroom door and watched Autumn putting on her clothes.

"Like I said, Autumn, you're not his slave, unless you wanna be," he said dead pan with cold eyes.

"Come on Rahjohn, please let's not mess up a good time, okay? I like you, I do, but we can't ignore the situation for what it is," she said, matter-or-factly, pulling up her skinny jeans.

"And what is it?"

Autumn stopped and looked at him with a smile playing subtly across her succulent lips.

"I had an itch, you had an itch and...we scratched. But now, I have to go back to my life and you have to go back to yours."

Rahjohn shifted uncomfortably, trying to adjust to a thought he'd never felt before.

That he was the brushee and not the brusher in this brush off.

"So, it's like that? Okay," he nodded, trying to mask his disappointment all the while keeping his male ego in place.

Autumn came over and wrapped her arms around his neck then kissed him softly. He didn't return the kiss. She sighed and looked into his eyes.

"Baby, believe me, my pussy is getting wet all over again, just thinking' about you. And real talk, I want to see you again. I just don't know when or how we can make that happen."

"I could arrest you," he chuckled, only half joking, "And then lock you in my little cage," he crooned.

"Sounds tempting," she replied then kissed him slow and sensually. When she broke the kiss, she added, "I'll call you."

Autumn slid it in so smoothly, as Rahjohn was so caught up in the moment, he failed to realize that was usually his line.

He walked her to her car. Autumn paused and turned to him inside the driver's door of the Corvette.

"Are you gonna try to follow me?" she asked.

Rahjohn smirked.

"And if I do?"

"When's the last time you've been in Philly?" she quipped, threw on the oversized Chanel shades and got in the car.

Rahjohn just chuckled and shook his head.

"Shorty is too much."

3:02 P.M.
HALLOWEEN

"Oh my God, Biz!" a heavyset, light skin girl gasped as Biz slowly got out the car, supported by one of his goons, his shirt soaked in blood.

The girl's name was Monica Childs Johnson and she was the daughter of Calvin Johnson and of Johnson's Funeral Home right off Farmers Boulevard. Calvin, who Bacardi's crew called 'Doc', had been a friend of Bacardi's uncle since they were kids. A Vietnam vet, he was also that hood doctor known in every ghetto that served as the ghetto medic when it was too dangerous to go to a real hospital. He had been patching up bullet wounds since 'Nam, through the crack era and through the Millennium, so Biz's wound may've looked bad, but Calvin had seen and healed worse.

"I'm good, I'm good," Biz grunted with effort. "Where your Pop's at?"

"He's inside waiting on you. Come on," Monica replied as she led Biz inside.

The four of them entered the back of the funeral home to find Calvin bent over a woman's cadaver, and injecting her with formaldehyde, while puffing a stubby cigar that had the whole room smokey.

"Yo, Unck man, come on. Put that stankin' ass cigar shit out, man. I got open wounds and shit, come the fuck on," Biz complained as Monica helped him get on a table directly across from the dead woman.

"Yo, can't you move her or something, cover the bitch up at least. I can't believe you got all this smoke up in here. I'm gonna get an infection," fussed Biz.

Calvin rubbed his bald head then washed his hands, speaking through clenched teeth. "Now you a goddamn doctor, huh? Nigga, sit yo' ass down and let me do what I do. You always come in this muhfucka crying, but got all the answers. If you know so much, how come you the one all fucked up all the time?"

Biz was in too much pain to argue with Calvin. Besides, he already knew how the old man was. A gangster, turned mortician. He still was a gangster at heart.

Calvin examined the wound and sucked his teeth.

"Aw nigga, that's what you called me for? I thought this shit was serious," Calvin commented as he cut Biz's shirt off. "Now I remember one night when Ronnie Bumps came through wit' his man. That nigga had so many holes; he looked like a slice of Swiss cheese. Bumps talkin' about, 'Cal, can you fix him?' 'Fix him?' I said. 'Bumps, if I can't, then you still brought him to the right goddamn place!'"

"Did you?" one of the goons asked. He had never been in Calvin's presence so he didn't know that the old man had war stories for days and that one question was all he needed to get him going.

Biz cut him off before he really got started.

"Unck! Goddamn, I'm bleedin' over here! Don't nobody got time to be listening to your life stories and shit while I'm over here dying. God damn, don't you see me in pain?"

Biz's phone rang. He struggled to reach it, so Monica unclipped it from his belt and handed it to him.

"Yo!"

"Where you at?" Bacardi asked, concealing his mounting fury.

"What up, B? Yo, I was tryin' to call you! Shit is crazy! Your man Grip..."

Bacardi cut him off. He had already heard about Biz's shoot out. That wasn't a priority to him.

"Whose wit you?" Bacardi probed.

"Dap and Malik. But..."

"Put Malik on."

"Biz felt a little uneasy with Bacardi's vibe. Something wasn't right. But he had no reason to think it was directed at him. He handed the phone to Malik.

Biz's mind was focused on the searing pain, and the stabs of pressure he felt from Calvin getting the bullet out. He didn't pay Malik any attention, nor did he see Malik's facial expression change.

"Bacardi said give me your house keys."

"What?"

Malik didn't repeat himself, he simply handed the phone back to Biz.

"Give him your keys," was all Bacardi said.

Something ain't right, Biz thought but he brushed it off and handed the keys to Malik.

"Fam, I'm tellin' you that nigga Grip..." Biz tried to tell him again, but Bacardi wasn't hearing it.

"Put Unck on the phone."

Biz never saw Calvin gesture to his daughter with his eyes to leave. If he did, maybe he would've recognized that something wasn't right in the room and that all eyes were on him. But his eyes were closed in pain.

In more ways than one.

Antoinette peeped at the policewoman subtly over her

shoulder and smiled. The policewoman's eyes were glued to 50 Cent's abs on TV, as B.E.T. played on the hospital screen. Antoinette returned her attention to the cell phone she had concealed under her pillow.

She texted:

Yo, time for some action!

A few moments later, she received:

You already know. I'm on her!

After sending a text message on her cell, Vita lowered her phone and fixed her gaze on the yellow Corvette that had just pulled up. The car itself was chromed out and turning heads on its own, but that wasn't what she was focused on. She was focused on the driver.

Autumn.

Vita hit speed dial and adjusted the Bluetooth to her ear, never taking her shaded eyes off of her target. Autumn's reflection played across the lens as she walked inside the hair salon.

"Where you, ma?" were Baby Wise's first words when he picked up.

"Merrick Boulevard and guess who I just saw?"

"Who?"

"Bacardi's bitch."

It was a short pause, short enough to be long. Vita could hear his wheels spinning.

"Stay right there."

Click.

By the time Bacardi arrived at the funeral home along

with Malik, Biz was groggy from the pain killer Calvin had given him. He forced his eyes to half staff when he saw Bacardi and Malik, Malik carrying a green bag.

"Yo Dunn, that nigga Grip had me set up. Nigga tried to kill me, Dunn, but just like Pac, I took it and smiled," he smirked.

Bacardi eyed him with a murder-flavored stare.

"And just like 'Pac, you won't get away the second time," Bacardi seethed.

"Huh?" Biz grunted confusedly. Did he hear him right or was it the medicine playing tricks with his mind? He didn't have long to wait for an answer.

Bacardi took the bag out of Malik's hand, unzipped it, then dumped seven kilos of heroin on Biz's bar chest.

"What the fuck?" Biz said, trying to sit up. "Yo B, what..."

"You tell me, nigga," Bacardi sneered. "This shit looks like the three birds I sold Baby Wise and the four I was frontin' him on consignment. And guess where I found 'em?! In your fuckin' hallway closet!"

"Wha...my... hell no!" Biz bellowed, the fogginess of the medicine instantly being erased from his mind and replaced by a higher alert sense of fear.

He struggled but sat straight up; just as Bacardi hooked him so hard he fell off the table and tumbled to the floor in a dazed heap.

"Ba...B...Bacardi, what the hell..." Biz stammered, struggling to get up. He made it to his hands and knees when Bacardi kicked him hard in his ribs.

"Don't even fuckin' say it, cocksucka! It was in your closet!" Bacardi barked.

"On my sister's grave B, I ain't have nothin' to do wit that!" Biz swore, gasping for air and holding his ribs.

Bacardi knew when Biz swore on his sister's grave, he was dead ass. But, he also knew a man faced with death

159

would say anything to save his life. So, just as quickly as he considered it, his anger blew it off as desperation.

"How'd it get there, Biz, how'd the fuck it get there? Wait, let me guess, Grip, the nigga you claim set you up, did that too?" Bacardi chuckled not wanting to hear the bullshit.

"Yes! I mean... no! I mean...I don't know..." Biz was talking so fast, his words tumbled over each other. "He...he had me...I don't know." He shook his head, then a vision of Antoinette shot through his head. "Antoinette?" he mumbled aloud.

"Nigga, save that bullshit," Bacardi hissed, looked at Malik and Dap, "Get his bitch ass up."

The two guns got Biz to his feet.

"Please B man, please! I swear it wasn't me! I swear! It had to be Antoinette," Biz blurted, ready to put it on anybody but himself.

"Antoinette?" Bacardi echoed in his face. "You expect me to believe your bitch set all this up? How she know if you ain't tell her? Don't worry, fam when the smoke clears, she'll be joinin' you."

Biz may've been in exasperating pain from the gun shot wound, but he mustered every ounce of strength he could trying to pull away from Dap and Malik. He knew he was about to die, but it was how he was about to die that petrified him. He knew Calvin had a crematorium and he also knew Barcardi loved deaden niggas in that shit. And judging by the look in Bacardi's eye that was exactly where he was headed, the crematorium.

"No! Please B, just shoot me! Please, anything but that!" Biz begged, struggling against the two guns.

"Light that motherfucker up," Bacardi told Calvin.

"Already waiting for you, nephew," Calvin nodded. When Bacardi had spoken to him earlier and told him to hold Biz there, he anticipated a problem.

"Please, Malik! Don't do this, man!" Biz's eyes were

160

wide with fear.

Malik felt guilty. After all, he was in Biz's crew. But Bacardi was the boss and besides he had found the bag in Biz's closet, so there was no doubt in his mind that Biz was guilty. Still, the look in Biz's eyes was saying something, but no one saw it.

"Shut the fuck up," Malik grunted, driving a punishing blow into Biz's jaw. He pummeled Biz several times, trying to have mercy on Biz and knock him unconscious. But Bacardi wanted to be merciless.

"Chill, Dunn before you knock him out," Bacardi sneered.

The blows had taken the fight out of Biz, but as they drug him into the room with the crematorium, he cried like a baby and pissed in his pants.

"B, I swear, I swear... I ain't do this shit. Please, if I gotta go, shoot me," Biz begged, looking in Bacardi's eyes.

Bacardi met his gaze firmly.

For the ultimate betrayal he would receive no less than the ultimate punishment.

Bacardi nodded and Calvin lifted up the furnace door. Usually, the metal slab in it slid out, and the body was place on that, but Malik and Dap didn't even bother. Biz struggled, but a blow to the solar plexus and testicles were enough to render him useless. They tossed his body into the furnace head first like a rag doll. Calvin slammed it shut behind him and turned up the flames.

The heat was felt by all of them, but that was nothing compared to the screams. Bacardi had heard it several times before. He still couldn't get used to the high pitch sounds of pure terror. Even Calvin flinched, but Malik and Dap looked sick. The screams weren't just high pitched, they were guttural, animal like and ear piercing. The smell of the human flesh roasting into oblivion even made Dap throw up. After a while, the screams stopped, but they continued to echo in their ears. Bacardi walked out and dialed Baby Wise's number.

Wise was sitting on the couch as he glanced at a number flashing on his phone. He smiled to himself, feeling like he had the upper hand. He had already sent a team to snatch Autumn up at the hair salon. He knew from there, Bacardi's life was at his fingertips. He decided to gloat, so he answered.

"What, nigga" Baby Wise snickered menacingly.

"Yo, fam, I..."

"Nigga, I ain't your fam."

Bacardi sighed.

"Look, I just called to tell you, I figured out what happened, and being the man I am, I'ma keep it one hundred. Biz set us both up."

"Biz?" Baby Wise laughed. "That's the nigga you gonna die over?! Didn't I tell you the nigga was foul? Wow, talk about somethin' comin' back to bite you in the ass, huh?"

Bacardi ignored his taunt.

"I got that yo, all of it and on the strength of me and you, I'ma charge it to the game. I'ma give you what you copped and I'ma give you what was gonna be on face, ai-ight?"

"And you think that's it?"

"Yo Wise, it's over! This ain't our beef! I handled that nigga and now I'm willing to walk wit..."

"You ain't letting me do shit!" Baby Wise barked. "Ain't shit over, you fuck ass nigga! You killed my man, you took from me and you tried to fuck my girl! Ain't shit over!

"Fuck your girl?" *This nigga's gone mad.* "Yo, fam, what the fuck is you talkin' about?" Bacardi quizzed.

"You ain't got nothin' else to tell me?"

"Huh?"

162

"You said Biz did this shit, right? But I'm saying, you ain't got nothin' else to tell me about snakes?" Baby Wise probed.

He wanted to see how sincere Bacardi was really being about squashing the beef. He knew if he told him about Grip, he was keeping it real across the board. If not, it was like he was concealing the fact in order to use it later. Now that distrust had reared its ugly head, it had snowballed to the point of no return.

"Yo man, I don't know what the fuck you talkin' about," Bacardi replied truthfully. He wasn't counting on Baby Wise knowing about Grip's treachery.

Baby Wise chuckled.

"Cool, just know this muhfucka, you wanna holla at my girl? Then I'ma holla at yours," Baby Wise hissed.

Click.

It didn't take Bacardi half a second to know exactly what Baby Wise was signifying. The only problem was, if Baby Wise was willing to put it out there like that, then he was planning something for Autumn and his heart sunk at the fear he was too late to save her.

Bacardi quickly hit Autumn on speed dial, while barking at his goons, "Let's go!"

The phone rang to her voice mail.

Autumn was in the salon, totally engaged in a humorous conversation with her stylist and one of the shampoo girls, as her phone began to ring. She looked at the number, it was Bacardi, but before she could answer him, three dudes in ski masks burst through the door, all three carrying pointed revolvers.

"Everybody get on the ground now! Get the fuck down!" one of them barked, as he snatched a woman from under the dryer and flung her to the salon floor.

The woman screamed and cried as two of the dudes ran up to Autumn, one grabbing her and putting his gun to the temple of her head.

"Please," she sobbed.

"Bitch, shut the fuck up," he hissed.

"Please, please don't hurt me," she begged.

"Shut up," he said tighting the grip he had around her arm, literally cutting off her circulation.

She nodded vigorously.

"Please don't hurt me," she said as the women in the salon sat helplessly watching the action-packed movie in living color.

He snatched her out the chair and began walking her to the door, gripping her fore arm with one hand while holding a gun to her side with the other.

"We walking out of here, nice and smooth, you got that, nice and smooth, bitch, nice and smooth."

"Where are we going?" she asked as if he would answer with truth.

"Shut the fuck up and stop asking questions," he barked as they exited the salon. Outside, a green van was double parked next to the Corvette with the sliding door open. The dude shoved Autumn inside then the three masked men jumped in, slammed the door and skidded off.

Vita picked up her phone and dialed a number.

"Done," was all she said. She disconnected the line, threw the phone on the passenger seat of the car and drove away.

Several minutes later, Bacardi skidded up in his Aston Martin, followed by Malik and Dap in a Suburban and three more goons in an Excursion. All three double-parked in the crowded lot as everyone got out, guns drawn. Bacardi remembered Autumn telling him she was going to the salon, so he double backed as quickly as he could.

He ran around the Corvette, visually inspecting it for any signs of damage then he ran inside the salon with his gun in his right hand by his side, followed by Malik and Dap. By the look on everybody's tear streaked face, he knew he was too late.

"Fuck!"

3:12 P.M.
HALLOWEEN

Rahjohn strolled quickly down the corridor of the 75th Precinct in Brooklyn. He took a wrong turn, double backed, made a right and walked in the side room of an interrogation room.

"You're late," said Morelli.

"Who died and made you boss?" Rahjohn quipped back as he opened a door and entered the interrogation room to find Natasha sitting across from a handcuffed Mellow.

"Sorry I'm late," he mumbled to Natasha as he sat down.

She leaned away from him subtly and rolled her eyes.

"Now, as I was saying, are you sure?"

"Sure? Ma, I'm posi..."

"Don't call me ma. I'm not your ma, got it? The name is Detective Bagley."

"Well Detective Bagley," he spat, like it was a curse word, "I'm positive. This whole shit was just like that."

"Fill me in," Rahjohn said with a question-like inflection tone at the end of his sentence.

"Mr. Davis was just telling me that the whole robbery was planned by Antoinette Jackson," Natasha explained, skeptically. She was thinking of everything Antoinette had told her. Her version seemed more plausible than the Mellow character that appeared before her.

Mellow could hear the skepticism in her voice, and replied to it. "Yo, I'm tellin' you, this bitch is mad slick! She was fuckin' my man Face, going behind her man back. So one day, she hollered at Face on some million dollar lick! The way it was planned, the shit was sweet."

"When you say 'behind her man's back', what do you mean?" Natasha asked.

"Just what I said, she ain't want that nigga to know about this. Hell, we was robbin' his man," Mellow replied.

Mellow didn't see himself as snitching because all of his team were dead. His mentality was how could he snitch on the dead? As far as Antoinette went, in his mind, she was an outsider. Not to mention, she killed Face and Tank and she deserved whatever she got for it. As far as he was concerned that bitch should be sitting there handcuffed to the chair instead of him.

"Who was the other girl?" Rahjohn probed.

"I don't know," Mellow answered.

"Was she a cop?" Natasha asked and Rahjohn looked at her briefly.

"I just said I don't know," Mellow repeated, "but she was a dark skin bitch with a fat ass."

"Can you describe her?" Rahjohn quizzed.

"Not her face, but I can describe that ass."

Rahjohn smirked at the comment.

I wish I could smack the stupid grin off his face. I swear I do. "Now you said that Face and Tank got $600,000 out of the hotel room and how many kilos of heroin?" Natasha asked, looking at her notes and keeping it professional.

"Eight, but we never got 'em. They still in the truck, I guess."

Natasha made a mental note to have the MPV torn apart.

"Where did the detective car come from," Natasha questioned.

"The Dominican on Atlantic, Sunrise Auto. They fixed it up."

"Are you sure Antoinette was the orchestrator?" she reiterated.

Mellow blew out an exasperated sigh.

"Look ma, I mean Detective, you want me to say somebody else set it up? Fuck it, tell me who YOU wanna pin this shit on and I'll say they did it. Other than that, I'm telling you everything I know!"

Rahjohn nodded and looked at Natasha.

"One more thing, does the name Autumn mean anything to you?" Natasha probed.

"Who?"

Natasha closed the file in front of her and stood up.

"Like I said, man, I ain't killed no cop. I did my part. Ain't no need for ya'll to play dirty," Mellow remarked.

"We'll be in touch," Rahjohn told him on the way out.

"I bet you will," Mellow mumbled.

Natasha and Rahjohn entered the observation room on the other side of the two-way glass, to find Morelli, Wakowski and Wilcox. Mellow sat in the other room, glaring at them through the glass.

"You're late," Wilcox growled at Rahjohn.

"I'm here now though," Rahjohn shot right back as he eyed Morelli.

"I think the monkey's holding out on us," Morelli remarked, eyeing Mellow through the glass.

Rahjohn ignored the comment and turned to Wilcox, "At least we got a line on who fitted the car out. Maybe we can get an i.d. on the other girl, Sunrise Auto on Atlantic

168

Avenue, see what they know."

Wilcox nodded and sighed in relief.

"And get the media off this 'dirty cop' angle."

"What about him?" Morelli pointed at Mellow. "That monkey shot a cop!"

Rahjohn turned to Morelli.

"First of all, he's no monkey. Secondly, we both know his dead partner killed Officer Mackey."

"Who says?! Him?! Whose fuckin' side are you on?!" Morelli sneered.

"Fuck you, Morelli," Rahjohn hissed.

"Fuckin' melanzane," Morelli mumbled under his breath, calling Rahjohn an eggplant, the racist term Italians use for Black people.

Rahjohn snapped. If it hadn't been for Wilcox grabbing him, he would've went straight to Morelli's ass.

"You fuckin' dick suckin', spaghetti-eating, muthafucka! Say it again!"

Wilcox restrained Rahjohn while Wakowski restrained Morelli.

"Get him outta here! I'll deal with him later!" Wilcox told Wakowski, who took Morelli out the door. Wilcox turned to Rahjohn. "And you! Calm your black ass down!"

"Me? Me? What about him? What? He don't think I know what a melanzane is? Piece of shit! It's cops like him that's the reason why I became a cop! Racist bastard!"

"You know how long I've been on the force, Griffin?! Do you? Nineteen goddamn years! I've seen more Morelli cops than you ever will, but I never lost my head! Never! You know what I'd do? I'd approach the guy nice and calm and ask him, why don't he and I go some place quiet after work and get it off our chest until one of us gives," Wilcox explained to Rahjohn, with steel in his eyes. "You know how many accepted my offer? One! One tough Irish son of bitch, but afterwards we never had a problem again! That's how you handle a racist muthafucka with a badge! You hear me?!"

"I hear you," Rahjohn grumbled as if a teenage boy once again.

"Now keep your eyes on the prize, like Bagley here. I like the way you handled that guy in there," Wilcox complemented her.

"Thanks chief."

The chief turned to Rahjohn.

"Anything on finding Bacardi?"

"No."

I thought that's where you were?"

Rahjohn sighed.

I was interrogating his girlfriend.

"And?"

"And? What do you mean, And? I interrogated her," Rahjohn huffed.

"Uh hmm and what did you find out?"

Short pause.

"Nothing."

"Nothing?" Wilcox echoed.

Rahjohn just looked at him. Wilcox nodded.

"Do like this," Wilcox said, holding out his right arm with his palm out, like he was stopping traffic, then he did the same with his left arm.

"Chief, I..."

"No, no, just try it... now get used to it, because if you tell me 'nothing' again, that'll be your new assignment. Are we clear?"

"Yes, Chief."

"Good."

Natasha and Rahjohn exited the Precinct and headed for their cars.

"So what did Antoinette have to say?"

Natasha continued to look straight ahead as she answered. "According to her, her boyfriend Biz set this whole thing up."

Thinking back to what Mellow said, Rahjohn asked, "So which do we believe?"

Natasha thought for a moment then responded.

"That's what I'm going back to the hospital to find out."

Rahjohn chuckled, at her use of 'I'. "What happened to 'we'?"

Natasha glanced at him out of the corner or her eye, but didn't say anything. They reached their unmarked and stopped.

"What's wrong with you, Tash? I said I was sorry for being late, okay? It's not that serious," Rahjohn said, fending off her attitude.

"You're right Rahjohn, it's not. It is what it is. So let's just wrap up this case and have it at that," she retorted, opening the door.

Rahjohn took her arm.

"Whoa, leave it at that? What's that supposed to mean?" he probed, detecting a strong finality in her tone.

Natasha studied him for a moment, then leaned toward him like she was going to kiss him. He misread her, so he leaned down to meet her lips, but she put her nose near his neck then leaned back, looked at him and said, "Chanel No. 5, right?"

The only thing more obvious than the pain in her eyes was the determination not to let it show.

She got in the car without another word being exchanged and drove away.

4:19 P.M.
HALLOWEEN

Vita, along side a green van, converged in front of a small, tan and white, single house on 231st Street. The van pulled deep into the driveway while Vita parked a few houses away. She got out the car keeping her eyes peeled as she approached the house. On the side of the door was a panel box. She entered a secret pass code then entered through the front door.

Inside the sparsely, dim lit, safe house, Vita's team had dumped Autumn's body on the living room floor, two guys with guns drawn stood above her.

Vita kneeled down beside her and grabbed a handful of her hair, pulling her head up and smirking in her face.

"Now, I don't swing like that, but you definitely a sexy mother fucka," Vita snickered. "I bet Bacardi'll do anything to get you back."

"Please, I ain't got nothin' to do with this," Autumn sobbed.

Vita ignored her and stood up as Baby Wise pulled up in an old Lincoln, then entered through the back door. He walked down the hall as he approached the living room. He

172

acknowledged the team, before kneeling down beside Autumn. He put the gun to Autumn's temple, cocking the hammer.

"Tell us how we can get at your man or die. Choose now," he gritted through clenched teeth.

"I will tell you," she whispered with a defeated tone in her voice.

"Smart girl," Vita remarked snidely.

Baby Wise took the gun from her head and speed dialed Bacardi.

Bacardi had tried Baby Wise several times and all he got was his voice mail. He automatically tried Grip, and his phone went to voice mail as well. That only confirmed what Biz had told him. Grip had set him up, and now that he had missed the hit on Biz, he was back safely in his own camp. Bacardi figured that while he was busy double crossing Baby Wise, Baby Wise was busy using the same pawn to triple cross him.

"Chess not checkers," he mumbled to himself as he paced the floor of Malik's apartment.

Chess indeed! And now Baby Wise had his Queen. Bacardi may've been ahead on the body count, but Baby Wise had upped the ante by snatching wifey. The thought of Baby Wise having the upper hand sent waves of rage ripping through his body, like electric jolts.

"Look, I been holding back on this nigga on the strength, like a father would do wit' his disobedient child," Bacardi hissed to Malik and Dap. "Cause I felt I could reason wit' the cocksucka, but no more! We gonna feed the streets dollars 'til it starts makin' sense, ya heard? Real talk, get at them stripper bitches over on Linden at Dazzle's, he loves that spot. Get at whoever you got to, just get me this nigga!" Bacardi barked like a drill sergeant.

173

His cell rang. When he saw it was blocked, he answered furiously.

"You fucked up, nigga! That's word on..."

"Nigga, shut the fuck up," Baby Wise based back at Bacardi. "I ain't wit' all that rah-rah shit 'cause you ain't gonna do a god damn thing! Now, you listenin' or should I just hang up and send this bitch's head back in a box?"

Bacardi fumed, but he kept his mouth shut.

"Ai-ight, that's more like it," Baby Wise snickered. He looked at Autumn, whispering to her as he used his hand to cover the receiver. "Yo, this nigga must love you for real."

"Nigga, just tell me what you want."

"I want you to listen."

"I am."

"Naw, listen," Baby Wise replied cryptically.

The next thing Bacardi heard was an ear piercing scream that made him grit his teeth against his powerlessness to do anything about it.

"You heard that? That was her pinky finger. Every half hour, I'ma cut off a body part, understood, unless I get three million large. Call me when you get mine, nigga. And remember, you only got twenty nine minutes left."

Click.

Baby Wise put the prepaid cell he was using in his pocket and looked at Autumn. Tears streaked her high cheek bones as she cradled her hand, sniffling. Baby Wise didn't really chop off her pinky finger, he just had one of his goons put a cigarette out on the back of her hand. That's all, she wasn't gonna die, not yet, anyway.

The phone in Baby Wise's pocket rang. He answered.

"Yo."

"Cocksucka done."

"Fall back."

Click.

The call came from the team he sent to Grip's

174

apartment. Once Baby Wise got confirmation that they had Autumn, he no longer needed Grip. Therefore, it was time to make him pay for his betrayal.

Grip didn't know Biz had been ambushed. He didn't even know he had been followed to the supermarket where he met Biz. All he thought about was getting something to eat and getting back to his nymphomaniac neighbor.

After hitting up his favorite Jamaican restaurant on Merrick Boulevard and copping an ounce of exotic, he went back to his crib.

The team was already waiting on him. They followed him upstairs and only made their presence known once they reached his floor.

"Yo Grip, what up?" One of the men greeted him in a friendly manner.

"Baby Wise wanna hollar at you," another told him as they entered his apartment.

They wasted no time pistol-whipping Grip then put one of his couch cushions over his face and shot through it three times to muffle the sound. The blood began to form around the back of his head and pool in a shape that resembled the African continent. They left the pillow over his head and were about to leave when they heard a knock at the door.

"Grip," his neighbor said, like the one word was her favorite song. The three men looked at each other. She knocked again.

"Come on, baby. I saw you come in. My pussy is drippin', but we gotta hurry before my husband..."

One of the men opened the door, startling her.

"Oh! Where's Grip?" she asked smiling flirtatiously with death.

"In the back," he said smiling back as he closed the door behind her.

She stepped inside and sealed her fate. When she saw

Grip's body and the pool of blood haloed around his head, the realization of what was about to happen to her hit her like Tommy from Goodfellas right before he got murdered. She didn't even have time to scream.

As the three men stepped over her twitching body, Grip's cell phone rang. Bacardi didn't know it, but he was calling a dead man.

The three men walked out, leaving the police two more murders to solve.

4:21 P.M.
HALLOWEEN

Rahjohn snapped out of his revelry when the horn from the car behind him loudly blew him back to reality. He was headed to Atlantic Avenue in Brooklyn, but his mind was headed a million miles away in a totally different direction.

He knew he wasn't doing right by Natasha. Hell, she was about to have his baby and truth speaking, she deserved more respect than what he gave her. She deserved a lot of a lot more than what he gave. He just didn't have it in him to give to her. But then again, she knew what he was about when they got together. And while they might be having a baby, everybody knows a baby doesn't make a relationship. He would be a good father, though. But in all honesty, he couldn't give Natasha what she asked of him, which was a relationship, especially now that Autumn had come into his life.

Autumn....

He just couldn't get her off his mind. He loved the way her hair flowed, her voice, her laugh, the way she moaned his name and the creaminess of....

He could feel himself rising to attention just thinking

about their episode together. But it was more than just sex with her. He could actually see himself getting into her, really putting time on that. He could even see exclusivity with her. Now, that didn't mean she'd be Mrs. One and Only but she could definitely move all the other females in his life back on the side line, way back on the side line. If only he could get Bacardi out of the picture. And he could get him out the way real easy; lock his ass right up. But, that wasn't his style. Rahjohn Griffin was a man's man, he was tough, but he always played fair, and he followed the codes of honor and integrity on all levels and with all people.

He pulled up to the Sunrise Auto garage. Salsa music blared from a loudspeaker affixed to the wall outside of the office. Several exotic cars sat around the entrance, and inside there was a souped up Porsche, a S600 and a Range all being worked on.

Rahjohn pulled up in his '03 Infiniti. One of the mechanics looked at the car and said, "Man, you don't need a garage; you need a junk yard,"

He and another guy started laughing and slapping high fives like shit was really funny to them. Rahjohn faked a chuckle then flashed his badge. Both of them stopped laughing immediately and their stupid smiles disappeared.

"Donde el Jeffe?" said Rahjohn in the little bit of Spanish he knew that got him by.

The mechanic pointed to the office where his boss was.

Rahjohn walked inside the office where a gum-popping Latina was speaking in rapid Spanish fire on the phone. Rahjohn approached the counter, but she didn't even acknowledge his presence.

"Excuse me."

She looked up, rolling her eyes.

"I'm on the phone."

Rahjohn pressed the clicker on the office phone and smiled.

"Not anymore."

"Hey, who the fuck..."

He flipped her his badge, but she didn't let up.

"...do you think you is? Fuck the fuckin' police! Like you run shit! You don't run nothing, hanging up my fucking phone, fucking cop!"

A middle aged Latin guy came out, hearing the word "police" and took Rahjohn in the back to his office.

"I'm so sorry Officer. Please come on in, what can I do for you?"

"Griffin, and actually it's Detective."

"Yes, Detective," the man said, extending his hand. "I'm Juan Ramirez. I run this place."

"You might wanna get a better secretary. I could've been a customer."

"I know, I know, but I didn't hire her for her people skills," Juan said, making his eyebrows go up and down. "If you know what I mean." Juan then sat down behind his desk. "What can I do for you, Detective Griffin?"

Rahjohn pulled out a few photos and laid them on the desk.

"Recognize that vehicle?"

Juan picked up the photos and shuffled through all eight of them. They were all of the Crown Victoria from the robbery, from different angles.

Juan held them out to Rahjohn.

"Can't say that I do," said Juan as he quickly shuffled through the pictures.

Rahjohn smirked.

"Why don't you look again."

"Detective... I'm sorry, I can't help you," he said smiling.

"Well, maybe I can help you." Rahjohn cut him off, leaned on the desk, hands flat against the surface. "Because I'm sure if I went through this place with a fine tooth comb I'd probably find, oh I don't know, serial numbers that don't jig with the vehicles, maybe a few illegals working here and if we..."

Now it was Juan's turn to cut him off.

"Maybe I can take a look one more time."

"I'd appreciate it."

Juan took another cursory glance at the top photo, sighed then flipped them on his desk.

"Yes, I remember this vehicle," he admitted then added quickly, "but I told them this would bring trouble."

"Told who?"

"I said to myself, 'who in the hell would want to ride around in a police car?' But, I no ask questions, you know what I'm saying? She was the girlfriend of a good customer. You know, so I say okay."

"She?" Rahjohn's ears perked up. He pulled out another picture of Antoinette. "Was this her."

Juan looked, and shook his head.

"No. Sorry, not her. This one very morena, eh, like chocolate."

Rahjohn remembered Mellow's words about her being dark skin.

"Okay, this good customer, what was his name?"

Juan shrugged.

"Ehhh, some guy from Queens. What's his name? He comes in all the time. His name is Baby Wise."

Rahjohn's eyes got wide.

"Baby Wise?" he echoed with confusion. "Are you sure?"

Juan nodded his head emphatically.

"Si, I see her come in a few times with Baby Wise then

180

she comes in on her own a couple of times. Then, maybe a week or so ago, she come with that car and tell me what she want. I no like it, but she pay me good." Then he let out a whistle and curved his hands in the air, the shape of a sexy girl. "Who can say no to those curves, eh?" Juan chuckled.

Rahjohn heard Juan and saw him flapping his hands around in the air, but Baby Wise was ringing in head. He was trying to fit this odd-shaped piece into a puzzle and it wasn't fitting or not yet, anyway.

"Thank you for your time, Mr. Ramirez. I'll be in touch."

"So, Detective Griffin, I do good? I help you, right?"

Rahjohn smirked.

"It's all good. Just don't bootleg no more police cars and do something about yappy your secretary, too."

"Si, si, detective, no more bootlegging and no more mean girls, right Abonia? You going to be nice to the police detectives from now on, si?" Juan asked as he patted her ass talking Rahjohn out the door and waving goodbye.

Rahjohn walked out, got back in his car and pulled off. As he drove, he thought about the bomb Juan the car man had dropped on him. If he was right and the other female was Baby Wise's girlfriend, then maybe he was focusing on the wrong side of the equation. He had been dividing when he should've been simply adding. Apparently, factors from both sides had come together, but under whose direction? Who would benefit? Mellow said, they had gotten six hundred thousand and there were supposedly eight kilos of heroin somewhere in the MPV.

That was chump change to Bacardi, but what about Baby Wise? Or could it be Antoinette's boyfriend? His final fleeting thought was, *was Antoinette and Baby Wise's girl in on this themselves.* It was too unbelievable. *Two girls, please. Think Rahjohn.* He quickly shook it off, not knowing how right he was.

He headed toward the hospital and texted Natasha.

Before he could put his cell back in his pocket, it rang in his
hand. Thinking it was Natasha calling him back, he didn't
even look at the caller ID display.

"Damn, you must be starving, huh?"

No response.

"Hello?" he said.

He looked at the display. It was Autumn.

"Autumn what's up?"

There was still no response from her, but he heard
voices in the background and what he heard made him slam
on the brakes.

As Natasha got off the hospital elevator on
Antoinette's floor, Rahjohn's text came in:

R ya'll hungry?

In spite of his bullshit, the text made her smile. She
knew the "ya'll" to which he was referring was her and the
baby. Natasha was so happy with herself for finally getting
pregnant she didn't know what to do. She was even happier
with Rahjohn, knowing that he was decent enough to be a
good father to her baby, even if he wasn't man enough to be
a husband. No matter what their differences, Rahjohn was a
fever she couldn't get over. And for Natasha, at the stage she
was at in her life, the other females didn't matter, as long as
she was carrying a part of him inside of her, nothing else
really mattered at all, except her baby. Deep down inside,
Natasha truly believed that fatherhood would change him,
and eventually they would all be together, like one big, happy
family. But, just in case her fairy tale romance didn't pan
out. It would still be okay, with or without Rahjohn Griffin, it
would be alright. Natasha was no body's fool. At the end of

the day, she was having her baby, because she desperately wanted a child. Natasha was thirty-three years old. Her clock was slowly ticking and she knew that she would never have a baby, if she was sitting around waiting for a husband first. In a way, she felt like she was using Rahjohn, but she was okay with that. If she couldn't have all of him, she'd always have a part of him, their child...her baby. It all would work out. Deep down, she could feel that they were destined to be together, destined to be a family.

She entered Antoinette's room just as she was finishing her lunch. Antoinette shoved the half eaten chicken and mashed potatoes to the side with disgust.

"I hope you got me some lunch, cause that shit is for the birds," Antoinette spat.

Natasha walked up beside Antoinette and told her, "Come clean with me right now or I promise you, you're on your way to Riker's Island infirmary and you know what I'ma say when you get there? Thanks Antoinette for all your assistance. You were a big help!"

"Come on ma, relax, you need me just like I need..."

"Need you!" Natasha retorted then laughed in her face. "That's what you thought? You over estimated yourself, Antoinette. See, what you didn't know is we have one of your co-defendants in custody too, Mellow."

A flicker of worry flashed through Antoinette's eyes that Natasha was sharp enough to catch. Then, it was gone and Antoinette's poker face was back in place.

Gotta give it to her, she's good, Natasha mused.

"And?" Antoinette answered with sass.

"And, he claims that it was you that put this whole thing together, not your boyfriend, just you," Natasha emphasized.

"Of course he's gonna say that, cause he never met Biz," Antoinette shot right back.

"No, you made it a point not to talk around Biz. How could you? You were robbing his man," Natasha smirked, using Mellows exact words against her.

Antoinette licked her lips with contemplation, then replied, "Look...fuck what Mellow say. It's what I say! Mellow can't give you Bacardi and Baby Wise on a silver platter, but I can. Don't forget what I told you ma-ma, I'ma make you famous," Antoinette winked mischievously.

"No more carrots on a stick, Antoinette. Give me the cop's name you said was involved," Natasha demanded.

"Not until you guarantee..."

"No guarantees, Antoinette. You're hangin' by my whim, now indulge me or the infirm..."

"Sonya Kirkland," she blurted out.

"What precinct?

"I don't know, somewhere in the Bronx?"

"Antoinette, I'm not playin' with you. If this is bullshit all deals are off."

'Whateva," she rolled her eyes. "Now can you go? It's time for my nap."

She rolled over, turning her back to Natasha.

"Sweet dreams," Natasha quipped sarcastically.

As soon as Natasha was gone, Antoinette turned over on her other side so that her back was to the officer. She pulled the cell phone from under the pillow.

She knew when Natasha ran the name Sonya Kirkland it would come up correctly because she really was a narcotics detective in the Bronx. Antoinette had caught a case a few years back and Kirkland was the undercover that arrested her. She had nothing to do with the robbery, but Antoinette just wanted to buy time. She knew, once she was on the Island, her peoples couldn't touch her so she texted with anxious aggression.

Yo! Where you at? I gotta move a.s.a.p.!

Vita snuck a peep at the incoming text. *We almost there baby girl!*

Autumn sat, huddled in the corner while Baby Wise paced the floor in front of her and his goons surrounded her in a half circle.

"Now talk, bitch, where the nigga at?" Baby Wise probed.

"I swear. He could be anywhere! I'll tell you the..."

Vita cut through the goons impatiently, and snatched Autumn by the coat collar.

"Y'all niggas is bullshittin'. I'ma show you how to make the ho spit!" Vita hissed, manhandling Autumn to the floor and throwing blow after blow.

"I'ma tell you. I'ma tell you!" Autumn screeched, balling up in a fetal position, but that wasn't all she did.

Seizing the opportunity while she was obscured from view, she reached in her pocket, fumbling for her phone until she was sure she felt the send button and double clicked it, sending the call to Rahjohn that made him slam on his brakes.

Vita stood over Autumn, breathing hard.

"Bitch, if he ain't at the first place you mention, I'ma personally ass fuck you with a curling iron, ya heard? Now where the fuck is Bacardi?"

"The brownstone in Harlem," Autumn replied quickly. "3112 140th Street."

Vita turned and smiled over her shoulder at Baby Wise.

"See how easy that was?"

Baby Wise looked at the goons.

"You heard the bitch, 3112 140th Street."

The goons hurried out. Vita started out behind them.

"Where you goin'?" Baby Wise questioned her.

She stopped, looked over her shoulder and replied, "Home. This war is over and you win."

185

Vita blew him a kiss and strutted out.

The first words Rahjohn heard was, "Ya'll niggas bullshittin'. I'ma show you how to make the ho spit!" in a female voice.

Right then, he went into action. He jumped out of his car, double parked and ran into the corner store, flashing his badge.

"Police! I need a phone!"

The Korean lady behind the counter quickly handed him the phone. He cringed inside when he heard the sounds of Autumn screaming, "I'ma tell you. I'ma tell you!"

He dialed Little frantically.

"Homicide, this is Lit..."

"Little, I need a GPS track on the number 5...55-1383. You got it?"

"555-1383. Got it. Wha..."

"No time, she's been kidnapped, and if we don't get there soon, they're gonna kill her!" Rahjohn bellowed.

"Kill her? Kill who? Wha..."

Click.

Rahjohn, in a haste walked out the store then remembered he still had the Korean lady's phone and handed it back.

"Thank you," he said, straining to hear what was going on with Autumn. He heard the guy screaming "where the fuck is Bacardi?" Then he heard Autumn give them the address. *3112 140th Street, Harlem.*

He knew instantly whoever had kidnapped her wanted to get Bacardi. They were going to kill him and now, Rahjohn knew where he was. He could easily contact the Precinct on 135th in Harlem and have them go and pick Bacardi up and save his life, but the question that popped into his mind was, who benefits?

Sure, he was a cop, sworn to uphold the law, to protect and serve, but what did that mean in the concrete? Protect Bacardi or serve the community by letting him face his fate? But if he ignored a potential homicide, turned his back, wasn't that breaking the law too?

Little beeped through on the other line, but he was scared to lose Autumn so he pressed ignore and ran back inside the store, snatching the phone from the Korean lady.

"Sorry," he apologized, hitting Little's number.

"231st Street, house number 1...6...6 dash 1...6. I've got dispatch on it already."

"Cool! Tell 'em not to make a move until I get there."

As Rahjohn jumped in his car, he made up his mind. He was a cop, Bacardi was a criminal, they were natural enemies. Whatever was about to happen, he had brought on himself. All of that was true, but the bottom line was Bacardi would be out of the way and Autumn could be his. That was reason enough to turn the other cheek to Bacardi's fate.

4:02 P.M.
HALLOWEEN

Bacardi came back downstairs in his Harlem brownstone and entered the living room where Dap and Malik were waiting for him. This was his main stash spot. A spot no one knew about, not even Autumn or so he thought. But now that Malik and Dap had been introduced to his hide out, he planned on getting a new ultra-secret spot.

He handed Dap the duffle bag he was carrying.

"That's five hundred large."

"But I thought you said Baby Wise wanted three million?" Malik questioned.

Bacardi sighed.

"Real talk, Dunn, shortie my heart, but three mill?" He shook his head. "That's a big number for a piece of pussy. But do what you can. Try to snatch the nigga that grabs the dough. Make him take you where she at. If not, it is what it is. That nigga's gonna pay regardless."

Malik nodded.

"That's what it is then."

He and Dap headed for the door. Dap turned back

around.

"You gonna be good here?"

Bacardi chucked arrogantly.

"Good? I'm always good. Besides, not even Autumn knew about this spot."

He walked them to the door and peeped out into the Saturday afternoon. Many kids were already getting a head start on their trick or treating. He smiled to himself, then turned and locked the door. He dialed Baby Wise. It went to voice mail after two rings. After he hung up, a blocked number called in. Bacardi knew it was Wise when he answered.

"They on their way."

"Lucky you, your time was almost up."

"How I know you won't kill her anyway?" Bacardi probed.

"You don't. But if you don't pay, I definitely will."

"Let me speak to her."

Short pause.

"Baby, please don't let them kill me!" Autumn cried.

The sound of her anguished pleas tore at Bacardi's heart.

"Baby girl, don't worry, I..."

"Happy now?" Baby Wise was back on the phone.

"Naw, but I will be when I see you," Bacardi gritted.

Baby Wise laughed and hung up. Then he looked at Autumn.

"You don't care about the money. You just wanna kill him. But what are you gonna do with me?" Autumn inquired.

Baby Wise looked at her with a curious look on his face.

"What do you think I'ma do with you?"

"I did what you asked me, Hakim."

"Yeah, and it damn sure ain't take long to get it out of

you," Baby Wise snickered.

"You think Vita wouldn't have done the same to you?" she shot back.

"Would you," he retorted.

Autumn lowered her eyes demurely.

"That was a long time ago, Hakim."

"Not that long. Besides, if you were still with us, you wouldn't be with me now?" he questioned.

As he studied her face, his mind went back ten years, and the pretty little sixteen year old he met on the 41st side of Queensbridge. It was Baby Wise that had taken her from rags to riches, not Bacardi. It was Baby Wise who taught her the 4 c's pertaining to diamonds: cut, clarity, color and carat. Baby Wise had taught her how to shoot a pistol, not like some inexperienced hoodlum, but with precision and accuracy. Much of whom she was, Baby Wise had molded in the three years they were together.

But it was also Baby Wise who had taught her the painful side of love, the possessive, insecure side, and as much as he tried, Autumn simply refused to be controlled.

It had been a crash and burn type of breakup, the only thing that cushioned the blow was the fact that Baby Wise had gone back to prison for a parole violation for eight months. The next time he saw Autumn, she was with Bacardi. This was the first time they had been alone since then, and all the unresolved emotions came rushing back to Baby Wise. He squatted down beside her and gently lifted her chin to look in her eyes. They could still mesmerize him like two liquid pools of emeralds that sparkled in the light.

"You never told him about us, did you?" he questioned.

"For what? There was no more us," she replied, holding his eye contact, knowing her gaze was hypnotic when she wanted it to be.

"I was young, you know. When I had you, I was too

young and reckless to know I had a jewel," he crooned, caressing her cheek. "You the only female I'd cut Vita off for. You say the word, and she's a wrap."

"And if I don't? Then you just gonna kill me, Hakim?"

He started to answer, but his words were cut short as gunshots erupted in the back yard.

Bacardi was just about to fix himself a sandwich when he heard it. *Is that my doorbell?* He had never heard the sound of it. That's how down low his spot was. Then he heard it again, it was a light buzz sound. Someone was definitely ringing his doorbell. At first he ignored it, thinking since it was Saturday, that maybe it was a Jehovah Witness. But then he heard the playful shrieks and giggles of children, and he knew it was trick or treaters.

He licked the Miracle Whip off of his thumb and made his way to the door. Bacardi peeped out the stained glass that framed each side of the door and saw the colorful little blurry outlines of costumed children. He opened the door to a Superman, an angel, a pirate and a cop, all looking about eight or nine years old.

"Trick or treat," they yelled in a broken unison.

"Ya'll lucky I like lil' kids," Bacardi chuckled, "but I ain't got no candy."

They all groaned, and Superman said, "Maaan, damn!"

"But I do have this." He held up a wad of bills, and the kids cheered like the Knicks had finally won a game.

He handed out crisp hundred dollar bills until he got to the kid in the cop's uniform. "Next year don't wear no shit like that, ya heard?"

The kid nodded emphatically, his eyes glued to the

hundred dollar bill Bacardi handed him.

Unfortunately, there would be no next year for any of them....

The Volvo parked in front of Bacardi's brownstone was stolen, and even though it looked empty, the three occupants were buckled down.

Too impatient to wait for Bacardi to come out, and worried that the longer they waited, the more likely the chance his people would come back, they did something drastic, cowardly, tragic. Noticing the few kids out early filling their bags, they paid superman, the angel, the pirate and the cop to ring Bacardi's bell. The rest was history.

The rapid fire stutter of the M-60 and the short bursts from the two AR-15s sparked brick, glass, skin and bones as the three gunmen suddenly spilled from the car and concentrated all their firepower at the porch. Had Bacardi been standing level with them, maybe, just maybe all of the bullets would've went over the children's heads and only hit Bacardi. But they didn't, and the gun men were so inexperienced that one by one the children fell to the ground, blood pouring from their tiny little frames.

Bacardi never got a shot off, never even got a chance to grab his gun. Thousands of dollars that had been knocked out of Bacardi's hands fluttered in the air as the four children and Bacardi's body jerked and twitched to the rhythm of the bullets. The whole block seemed to be paralyzed by the sixty seconds it took for the hit to be done, then the Volvo skitted out of view. Blood covered the children and Bacardi as it dripped down the steps. The angel, a young eight year old stared blankly into the sky, her eyes like soulless windows needing to be closed. In those sixty seconds Halloween had become a gruesome bloodbath in Harlem.

"What the fuck?! I said, nobody move until my word,"

Rahjohn barked, crouched behind his car, one house down from where Baby Wise was holding Autumn.

He had been in the process of carefully setting a perimeter around the house when he heard the shots ring out. What he didn't know was the shots hadn't been initiated by an officer but had actually come from the gun of one of Baby Wise's goons.

Two goons had been posted in the back of the house in case of an ambush. When they saw the police officer trying to slip through the bushes from the adjoining backyard, they didn't ask questions, they simply shot first. The police, surprised to be under attack, responded with deadly force, killing one of the goons, while the other fled around the side house.

As the police tried to move on the front of the house Baby Wise was on guard and sent several shots at them through the living room window. The police scattered then thirty seconds later returned fire heavily through the living room.

Rahjohn ran down the street yelling and screaming at the other officers. "Hold your fire! Hold your fire! He's got a hostage! Cease fire, he has a hostage!"

The second goon that fled the backyard ran right into a nest of S.W.A.T. officers.

"Drop your weapon."

"Get down!"

"Now!"

"Don't move!"

The conflicting orders had the paranoid youngster not knowing what to do. First, he dropped the weapon then put his hands up. Seconds later he was tackled to the ground and cuffed.

Rahjohn took cover behind the corner of the house.

"Baby Wise! This ain't how it's gotta go down, Brah! Be easy and we can all walk away for this in one piece,"

Rahjohn bellowed, trying to soothe the nerves Baby Wise probably had frazzled inside.

The response he received was music to his ears.

"Rahjohn, I'm in here," Autumn cried out.

"Baby!" he blurted out, before catching himself. "Autumn, are you okay? Where's Baby Wise?!"

"I'm okay, I'm okay!" she sobbed. "He's on the floor. The blood... I don't know," she stammered, her voice breaking up with tremors.

Rahjohn looked through the front window of the house and could see Baby Wise lying on the floor.

"He's down," Rahjohn barked.

Seconds later, the battering team was on the porch, knocking down the door. Rahjohn was the fourth man in.

"Get down on the floor!" an officer screamed at Autumn, gun aimed at her. Two more went to check the rest of the house. Autumn began to comply until Rahjohn broke through.

"It's okay! She's not the perp!" Rahjohn told the officers. They lowered their weapons.

Autumn embraced Rahjohn tightly, crying into his chest.

"You okay?" he asked intensely.

She nodded, wiping her eyes.

"I... I was scared, baby. I was really scared," Autumn sobbed.

Rahjohn was really self-conscious with Autumn calling him "baby" around the officers.

"Come on, let's get outta here," he suggested, putting his arm around her shoulder and walking out.

Rahjohn eyed Baby Wise's dead body sprawled on the floor, his body laying under the window, his blood soaking into the dirty grey carpet, the sun shining across his ashen face highlighting his deadly stare that was frozen in eternal surprise.

194

There was just something about the scene that didn't feel right, but he shrugged it off for the time being. The next time he would remember, it would be too late.

As he walked her out, he looked straight into Natasha's face as she got out of the police car, with Wilcox in an unmarked behind her. He diverted his gaze, feeling guilty for a reason he couldn't quite put his finger on.

He walked Autumn over to the ambulance then headed to Wilcox and Natasha. He avoided her accusatory glare and focused on Wilcox.

"So we got 'em?" Wilcox asked.

Rahjohn nodded.

Wilcox sighed with relief. "Well... hopefully this thing is over. Bacardi can't go to war with himself," Wilcox remarked.

"Now we just need to tie up the loose ends on the robbery end of this thing," Natasha said. "Antoinette gave me the name of a cop she said is involved, Sonya Kirkland. I was just about to check it out when I heard about this."

"What's her connection?" Rahjohn probed.

"She says she's the second girl, the one posing as the detective," Natasha answered.

"She's lyin'. I went by Sunrise Auto and found out who our mystery woman is. You'll never guess," Rahjohn informed them.

"No I won't, so just tell us," Wilcox retorted impatiently.

"Baby Wise's girlfriend."

"Baby Wise's girlfriend?" Natasha echoed, frowning. "But if she and Antoinette are in cahoots..." Her face brightened with the light of comprehension. "Wow."

"Exactly," Rahjohn said.

The medical examiner wheeled Baby Wise's body out in the standard black bag on a gurney.

"Look at that," Wilcox commented with disgust. "No

matter how long I'm on the force, I'll never get used to seeing that."

"What, a dead body?" Natasha asked.

Wilcox shook his head.

No...another dead Black man. Baby Wise may've been a low down, dirty piece of shit dealer, but now he's in one of those bags. That's all he'll ever be. We've lost another one," Wilcox said solemnly, then clapped on both Rahjohn's and Natasha's shoulder.

"Great job, kids. Now let's bring it home."

Wilcox went inside the house, ducking the crime scene tape, disappearing inside.

"How did you know?" Natasha asked, nodding in Autumn's direction.

"She called me, so I used GPS to track her," Rahjohn explained.

"Smart girl," Natasha quipped, and Rahjohn knew she meant more than just the phone call.

Before he could say another word, Autumn walked over.

"Umm," she spoke timidly. "The officer said I was free to go. And if it isn't too much trouble..." she began to ask, as Rahjohn completed the question with an answer.

"Yeah, no doubt," he replied then turned to Natasha. "Uh, Tash, I'ma take her home real quick, ok? Then I'll meet you at the Precinct."

"Okay, Rahjohn," Natasha replied blandly, then walked off.

Taking note of her reaction, Autumn asked, "I didn't interrupt anything did I?"

In more ways than one, Rahjohn thought to himself.

"Naw, come on, I'll take you home."

Natasha watched them walk to Rahjohn's car. How he

opened the door for her, how he helped her into the car. It all hit Natasha on a primal level and made her boil. As they pulled off, despite her self, she decided to follow them.

Rahjohn drove her home, to the townhouse she shared with Bacardi, in an awkward silence. He asked her repeatedly was she okay, and repeatedly she answered yes. Other than that, not one word until they got to the townhouse.

Can you come up with me?" Autumn offered.

Rahjohn looked her in the eyes.

"Ma, I don't know if that's a ..."

She gripped his hand.

"I just don't want to be by myself right now, Rahjohn."

Still... the obvious remained unsaid. Both of them were hoping that Bacardi was dead, and they both knew the other was hoping the same. But for some reason, Rahjohn felt hesitant. Like finally attaining something you know you shouldn't have, then feeling guilty because you got it. He had purposely ignored a murder for what he saw Autumn offering, yet now he hesitated at the threshold....

Moment of honesty,
Someone's got to take control...who's it gonna be?

Even though there was no music playing as they entered the apartment, Alicia Keys was singing "I'm ready" in the background. Autumn took off her coat and laid it across the back of the couch.

"You want something to drink?" she offered.

"Naw, I'm good," he declined.

"You sure? Oh, I forgot, you're on duty," she remarked, then giggled nervously.

Rahjohn stepped closer.

"Autumn, you sure you're okay? A situation like that would have anybody shook up."

197

Autumn took a deep breath then perched on the arm of the couch, one leg tucked behind the other.

"I don't know, how am I supposed to feel? Angry, scared and relieved all at the same time? It's just crazy," she told him, diverting his gaze.

He lifted her chin and smiled into her eyes.

"It's okay. It's over. Now, it's all over."

She studied his face for a moment. "Are you mad at me?"

"Why would I be mad at you?"

She shrugged, got off the couch arm and brushed past him.

"Because, it's like you told me that this could happen, something like this and I didn't listen to you. Now look what happened. I could have been murdered." Her voice trailed off and she wrapped her arms around herself like she was cold.

Rahjohn went to her and gently turned her face to him.

"Ay, don't do that to yourself. It ain't your fault."

"I'm not sayin' it's my fault. It's just," she looked into his eyes with the innocence of a child. "What you think of me matters, so tell me are you mad at me?"

He smiled, kissed her forehead and answered, "No. I'm not mad at you?"

Her face brightened with an alluring smile.

"If we could start over, right here, right now could you overlook who I was and focus on all I could become?"

I was wonderin' maybe...
If I made you my baby...
If we did the unthinkable, would it be crazy...

"I accepted you for who you were the minute I laid eyes on you. But what are you askin' of me?"

"A chance," she whispered, then gently kissed his lips.

or would it be so beautiful...

Rahjohn returned the kiss, then looked her firmly in the eye. "Even if he's not dead?"

Deep down, they both knew Bacardi was dead, or at least they sincerely wanted to believe that he was. But Rahjohn's ego needed to know, even if Bacardi walked through the door right then and there, that Autumn would still choose him.

There was no hesitation in her response.

"Even if he's not dead."

...either way I'm sayin' if you ask me I'm ready....

The first time they fucked it was the type of raw animal lust that mingles pain and pleasure in one passionate embrace. But this second time was different. Rahjohn undressed her slowly. For every part of her body that had been covered with clothes, he covered with kisses. He laid her down on the thick carpet, running his tongue up the inside of her calf all the way to her navel, then took her clit in his mouth and sucked it gently.

"Rah," Autumn gasped, arching her back and digging her nails into the carpet above her head, "Don't stop."

The varying pressure he put on her clit, sucking lightly then harder, had Autumn cumming in his mouth before she knew it, as she moaned his name in ecstasy.

"Put it in me, baby, put it inside me," she panted, urging him up. He kissed up her belly to her nipples, nibbling and sucking them, making her tingle with pleasure. Autumn gripped his thick dick and guided it inside of herself, then wrapped her legs around Rahjohn's waist.

"Sssssssss, yeah baby, right there," she groaned wistfully as Rahjohn long dicked her pussy slow and sensually.

Autumn rolled Rahjohn over on his back and mounted him like he was a stallion. Placing her hands on his chest, she leaned forward then began to grind and twist, biting her bottom lip.

"Damn, I love the way you ride this dick," Rahjohn grunted, palming her ass and pushing himself deeper.

"Yeah?"

"You love it?"

"I love it."

"I love you," she cooed as her pussy exploded on his dick.

"I love you too," he admitted, and for the first time in his life, he meant it.

He came deep inside her, then she leaned down, covering his face with kisses.

"Don't hurt me," she said, the vulnerability in her eyes on full display.

His answer was a reassuring embrace that hurting her would never happen.

5:47 P.M.
HALLOWEEN

She had to know. She just had to and she had to see for herself with her own two eyes.

She had been sitting in the parking lot of Autumn's townhouse for close to two hours, and her patience was wearing thin. But still she had to know the truth.

The last slivers of sunlight had long disappeared. Natasha had been watching the comings and goings of trick-or-treaters all evening. She was tired and hungry. *I thought you were meeting me at the Precinct.* Natasha stared at the front door as if she had x-ray vision. She could only imagine what was going on inside. And to say the least, her imagination had her blood boiling. By any sane man's standards, she was beautiful. She may not have had the vivacious body of a video vixen, but she was shapely, toned and well proportioned. She couldn't understand why Rahjohn would choose Autumn over her. Thoughts of *what's wrong with him* slowly became, *what's wrong with me?* Rejection plays havoc on one's self esteem. She had seen Rahjohn run through a bevy of women. But she saw it, no better yet, she felt it, when he looked at Autumn after the kidnapping. She wondered what it was about men that made them so blind to the good woman standing right in front of their face, but break their necks for the no good chick on the corner?

Just thinking of that, the life inside of her and picturing what she knew they were doing inside had her so hot she was ready to kill something or somebody.

The door opened and Autumn walked Rahjohn out. Their eyes were focused on each other, so they didn't see Natasha approaching them. As much as he didn't want to, Rahjohn knew he had to go. He hadn't meant to stay as long as he had.

"Puff is throwing a masquerade tonight. Will you take me?" Autumn proposed.

"Eh, don't know, baby, the case has..."

"Please Rahjohn, I really want to go. I'll make it worth your while," she flirted.

"Oh yeah?"

"Oh yeah," she replied, with a kiss.

"What time?"

"Pick me up at midnight," she said gently kissing his lips.

Neither one of them paid any attention to the thud of a car door slamming.

"And listen baby, I know it won't happen overnight, but I'ma need you to phase all of this out. I mean everything having to do with Bacardi. You understa..."

"You switched sides, huh?! You fuckin' her? What else you got going on, huh?" Natasha screamed on him, mushing him in the chest and literally pushing Autumn out the way.

"Natasha! What the fuck?! What are you doin' here?" Rahjohn replied, surprised and totally off guard.

"I would ask you the same thing, but it's obvious what the hell is going on, Detective Griffin," Natasha spit, her tone laced with accusation and sarcasm.

She tried to push him again, but he grabbed her arms. Natasha yanked away.

"Bitch, what the fuck are you lookin' at? You think you're so goddamn cute, don't you? I'll tell you what's cute! How he's using you to get at your boyfriend! Snitching for the dick," Natasha laughed wildly. "Go head, Rahjohn! Tell her!"

Autumn stood there, shaking her head, thinking it's a shame what good dick will do to you.

"What the fuck you shaking your head for? Rahjohn, you not gonna tell her?"

"Natasha, why the hell are you acting like this?" Rahjohn barked on her.

Natasha knew she was making a fool of herself, but she was past the point of caring.

"No! Why are you actin' like this?" Natasha shot right back at him, then turned to Autumn with a smirk. "You know, I'm having his baby, right? Oh, he ain't tell you? Well now you know," she spat, her tirade beginning to wind down, as the tears of hurt and disbelief welled up.

"Natasha," Rahjohn said, soothing her. "Listen..."

"Did you kill him yourself," Natasha blurted.

"Kill who?" Rahjohn questioned. *Tash is really tripping.*

"Bacardi! You think I can't see it?! How conveniently she called and almost at the same time they all got killed in Harlem," she shook her head.

"They?" he echoed.

"They! Bacardi and the four little kids who were all gunned down, four children dead along side Bacardi," she spat.

What she told him hit him like a bullet.

"Four kids?" he mumbled and staggered slightly. His head was spinning wildly.

Four kids?

203

"I...I gotta go," he said, glancing at Autumn.

"Rahjohn, you gonna be okay?" Autumn asked but received no answer.

He jumped in the car and skidded off.

Autumn and Natasha eyed one another coldly.

"This ain't over," Natasha sneered as she walked away.

"You're right, it's not," Autumn whispered to herself, then turned on her heels and went back inside.

Rahjohn was halfway to the Tri-Borough Bridge before he realized it was pointless. The only thing driving him was guilt, but the thought of having to look the parents of the dead children in the face sickened him with shame. He pulled over and cut the car off, then rested his forehead on the steering wheel.

"Damn," he muttered to himself. *Not four children dead.* A grotesque image of automatic weapons tearing through the flesh of the small children as if he had been there to witness the shootings with his own eyes, flashed through his head. He wished he could get away from himself. Truth is no matter where you go, there you are.

The media would say they had been victims of a drug war, a gang-related killing. But they would be wrong. They were the victims of Rahjohn's hatred of Bacardi and desire for Autumn.

"I knew and I did nothing. I fuckin' knew," he whispered angrily, banging the hood of the car with his fists. "Had I just done the right thing," he said not even noticing the people walking by glancing in his direction. They hurried along not wanting to get in the way of the crazy Black man banging on his car, talking to himself. He squatted on his haunches in front of the car, the glare of the headlights illuminating his guilt. He sat down on the ground, knees up and elbows encircling them

"I can't believe what I let happen. I can't believe myself. I didn't do..." He shook his head, feeling tears refusing to let them from his eyes. "...nothing, not a goddamn thing!" He felt so ashamed and so sorry for the four young souls. *If only I could chose again.* He knew he would one day have to answer for his reasoning.

"Mira, mami! Lookin' gooood!" the Spanish mechanic cat-called as the thick, chocolate chick with the blond wig on entered the office of Sunrise Auto. That's what he would remember later when the police would ask.

"Yeah, a Black chick, but, eh, blond."

She entered the front area where the secretary usually waited behind the counter, but Abonia wasn't there. She strutted down the hall and Juan's ooh's and ahh's got louder.

"Ay dios mio!"

She opened the door and found Juan sitting on the edge of the desk with his pants around his ankles and the secretary on her knees sucking his dick.

"Hey, what do you think you're doing? Wait outside!" Juan grunted.

She raised her silencer-equipped Heckler and Koch.

"Don't worry, this won't take long," she retorted smoothly, then squeezed off a round into the back of Abonia's head, blowing Juan's secretary's brains all over his naked mid-section. Her body slumped into Juan's crotch, his dick still in her gaping mouth until he pulled her off and started hyperventilating.

"No, no! Don't kill me! I tell the police nothin'," he lied.

"And you won't either," she said, squeezing off two more shots that hit Juan in the head and chest, knocking

205

him off the desk. She came, stood over him then put two more in his face for good measure.

Vita looked in the mirror behind the desk, adjusted her wig and walked out, having one more stop to make. She parked her car and grabbed her cell phone from out of her purse.

What's the combination?

Vita texted, then almost immediately received:

28-16-3 hurry up bitch!

Vita opened Biz's safe and a smile spread wide across her face. She knew it wasn't as much as she had just emptied out of Baby Wise's safe, but stacks and stacks of money always made her smile. It would turn out to be one point seven million, just over half of the two point nine million Baby Wise had. She threw the money on the bed, stack after stack, then tied the bed sheet in a big knot. She texted Antoinette:

Bitch, calm ur ass down b4 we leave ur ass!

Vita smirked as she sent the text. There was no way she would leave Antoinette. She was a part of the team. They had pulled this off together. The game was over. There was no one left to track them down. The plan had been a total success.

How gangsta was it that they had orchestrated the robbery in order to turn Bacardi and Baby Wise against one another, at the same time pulling the strings behind the scene. All they had to do was get the ball rolling, then step back and let the animosities, the jealousies and larcenous hearts take over. It was a plan to put emotion over intellect, but what was ironic was that it was the men who were emotional, while the women won through intellect.

Vita drug the bundle of money off the bed with a grunt. It was close to fifty pounds. She pulled the bundle to the car, threw it into the back next to the three duffle bags full of Baby Wise's money.

One more stop to get Antoinette then it would all be over. She could almost feel the Caribbean breeze.

7:03 P.M.
HALLOWEEN

It's a thin line between love and hate, and Natasha was teetering on that line. In her mind, Rahjohn had humiliated her, although in reality she had humiliated herself.

She wanted, no she needed to hurt him as much as he had hurt her. The thought of terminating the pregnancy went in and out of her thoughts. *Should I do this.*

With tears streaking her cheeks, she decided to terminate the pregnancy. But, as quickly as her mind was dead set against him and his baby, her heart sang a different song.

Her cell phone rang.

"Yes...okay, you're sure? And she's logged for that time? Thanks, Little."

Natasha hung up then shook her head to clear it. She had to get her head back in the case. What Little had told her confirmed what Rahjohn said. Sonya Kirkland, the Bronx narcotics detective Antoinette had told her about, had checked out. She had been in an interrogation during the time of the robbery. Her name was in the precinct log, which meant Antoinette had lied, which meant Antoinette was on her way to Riker's Island.

Without hesitation, she called Rahjohn. Regardless of

208

their personal issues, they still had a case to solve. Besides, they were partners.

For now.

A few minutes before Natasha rang in, Autumn had called first. Her call is what brought him back from his stupor. He heard the phone ringing and it made him think of life, life still lived. He got up, got in the car, and picked up his phone.

"Yeah."

"Baby, you okay," Autumn inquired, hearing the clouds in his voice.

"I'm good," he lied.

"Well, you sort of had me worried, the way you left, and all."

"I said I'm good, ma," he snapped, brashly.

"Oh what, I'm not supposed to care? You wanna spaz on me 'cause I'm concerned?" she asked with an edge in her tone as well.

He sighed.

"Yo, my bad, Autunm. I'm just stressed. I...." He wanted to tell her about the children and what he knew but he couldn't.

"Listen, baby, let's skip the Puff thing, okay? Why don't you come back over and I'll cook you whatever you want," she offered.

"I like the sound of that."

"I thought you would, so you on your way?"

Rahjohn checked his watch, then answered, "Yeah, no doubt."

She blew a kiss through the phone.

"I love you," she sang.

"I love you too."

Then where's my kiss?"

"Huh?"

"I gave you one, where's mine?"

He chuckled then sent her an air kiss and hung up, smiling. Autumn definitely knew how to cheer him up. When he started to pull off, his phone ran again.

"Yeah."

"You were right, that Bronx detective? It was a dead end," Natasha told him.

"Then we need to lean on Antoinette, convince her she's covering for Baby Wise's girl, and let her know she's gonna be the one to wear it."

"Exactly where I'm headed now."

"I'm on my way."

Rahjohn pulled off and headed for Brooklyn.

They arrived at the hospital at the same time. Rahjohn got out of the car and approached Natasha. He wanted to apologize, to set things straight, but he knew this wasn't the time.

For Natasha's part, her stomach was in knots of mixed up emotions just being around him. Several times between the car and Antoinette's room, she started to blurt out, "I'm getting an abortion," but she didn't, she knew she didn't mean it. They rode up on the elevator, cutting glances at each other, pretending to watch the numbers above the elevator door.

They got off on Antoinette's floor, and the first thing they noticed was that there was no officer outside of Antoinette's room. The fact wasn't alarming in and of itself. Both officers may've been in Antoinette's room, or more than likely, somewhere they weren't supposed to be.

Rahjohn was right on both assumptions.

Both officers were in Antoinette's room and somewhere they weren't supposed to be: face down, one on

210

the floor, the female officer slumped over the bed, eternally resting in puddles of blood, and still twitching involuntarily. Antoinette was gone.

"What the hell?" Natasha gasped, drawing her weapon.

Rahjohn pulled his as well, quickly checked the bathroom. Then they both ran out of the room.

"Alert security! Officer down in the room! Move!" Rahjohn barked at the nurses as he and Natasha headed for the stairs.

They moved swiftly but cautiously down the stairs, guns poised. They knew the only possibility was the stairwell. They certainly hoped they were in the building.

They were right.

As they rounded the stairs heading for the third floor corridor, they spotted a nurse with a female patient. The female patient had her arm around the nurse's neck, and the nurse had her arm around the patient's waist for support. In the nurse's left hand was a silenced Heckler and Koch.

"Drop the weapon now!" Natasha barked.

She was the first to enter the corridor and had the drop on Vita and Antoinette. They froze just as Natasha heard the scariest sound she'd ever heard as she felt the coldness of steel on her temple. The sound was the cocking of a .38 snub and the coldness of the barrel, her death only three inches away.

"No, you drop yours."

Rahjohn rounded the corner a split second after Natasha, but even he was too late. He saw the gun and heard the voice, rounding the corner as he couldn't believe what he saw.

"What the fuck? Autumn, what are you doing here?" he based, totally confused, his stomach doing acrobats.

Autumn, dressed as a nurse as well, had her gun to the back of Natasha's head, while she smoothly removed the gun from Natasha's hand.

"Trick or treat, sweetness, like my outfit?" she smirked.

Inside, Rahjohn was reeling as his perception came to grips with reality.

"You!" was all he could get out, aiming his gun at Vita then Autumn, then back again at Vita.

"Moi," she snickered, saying the word like a kiss. "Now put it down, or I splatter your baby mama."

"You don't have to do this, Autumn," Rahjohn said authoritatively, trying to calm his fluttering heart.

"I'ma count to five,... three... four..." Autumn warned, her voice taking on a street-ness he had never heard.

Rahjohn slowly put his gun on the floor and raised his hands.

"Baby, listen, don't let these two drag you into this, okay? Let me help you."

Autumn laughed in his face.

"Drag me into this? Yeah, you really are lost. Look at his face, Vita," Autumn giggled.

"That nigga sick, boo," Vita cracked, and the three of them laughed at Rahjohn's naivety.

"It was all a dream," Antoinette sang, using Biggies words.

"You been played playboy, and you fell for it, hook, line and sinker. You know why," Autumn asked rhetorically, with a shrug! Didn't you notice I didn't talk to you until Antoinette got shot? I needed you, to stay in your ear, make sure you kept her here, so we could get at her. Now, I don't need you anymore."

Rahjohn was still trying to wrap his mind around it all.

"But they kidnapped you," he mumbled, then like a picture coming into focus, it all made sense. He knew why the kidnap scene didn't feel right.

212

He could see Baby Wise lying on the floor, his head toward the window, in a pool of blood. He hadn't been shot from the outside. He had been shot from the inside...

By Autumn.

Autumn had indeed shot him. It was planned that way. They used the kidnapping so Autumn wouldn't be around when the hit went down on Bacardi. At the same time, she was supposed to kill Baby Wise. That's why Vita had tussled with her and threw punches: to give Autumn time to reach her phone and for Vita to slip her the gun. While she curled up in the fetal position, Vita was giving her the gun.

When she pulled it and shot Baby Wise point blank, center forehead, he was so shocked, he died with that expression on his face, the eternal expression of surprise.

"You know, Rahjohn, I thought you'd be harder to fool, but you weren't. Hook, line and sinker, you fell for my game," Autumn giggled.

Autumn kissed Natasha on the cheek.

"You were right, boo, it wasn't over, but it is now."

"Rahjohn," Natasha pleaded, her eyes full of fear. All she could think of was her baby, her life and the life she had hoped for with him. She didn't think it would happen like this, not like this.

Boom! Boom!

The .38 echoed through the hallway as she blew a hole in the back of Natasha's torso, piercing her vest. Natasha collapsed to the hospital floor.

"Nooo!!" Rahjohn bellowed.

Vita raised her gun and squeezed off three in his chest and right shoulder.

Usually, he would have been wearing a vest, but he didn't put it back on after his escapade with Autumn. The force of the blast pushed him back against the wall then he pitched forward, on his face not even five feet from Natasha's

213

unseeing eyes. The blood on the wall ran down for three spots almost in a perfect triangle where all three bullets went through him.

"See? If you could've just went to my house and waited, you'd still be breathin'. I tried to save you," she shrugged convincingly.

Everything seemed so far away. The sounds, the lights, even the pain in his chest. He felt disconnected from him. He knew why. He was dying. He looked at Natasha, and could see her standing there asking him 'why'.

I'm sorry, Tash, I'm so sorry. He looked at her lifeless like body laying still, blood pouring from her chest.

As he watched the three females walk away and disappear through the exit door, he realized that he didn't hate Autumn for what she did. They say you can't help who you love, and even lying on the floor soaked in blood, he couldn't help but love Autumn.

The last thought he had was an old song his mother used to play.

Everybody plays the fool...
There's no exception to the rule....

Then everything faded to black.

11:02 P.M.
Halloween

"Yes, Steve, it has been a very bloody Halloween indeed. In less than twenty four hours, a drug war that police say began in Queens has taken dozens of lives including one of New York's largest heroin suppliers, four tiny young trick-or-treaters in Harlem, and several police officers. Police say that a woman dressed as a nurse shot and wounded two detectives while on duty. The suspect dressed as a nurse snuck into the hospital to help break out another suspect who was under police custody. They made good on their escape, but in a strange twist, both women were found dead, shot execution style in an SUV in the hospital parking lot. Police are not sure who the assailant is, but the manhunt continues, back to you, Steve."

The newswoman turned and looked over her shoulder at the yellow police tape strung around Vita's powder blue Mercedes jeep. All four doors were open. Vita and Antoinette laid on opposite sides of the jeep with white sheets over them. A few hundred dollar bills littered the ground around them as the crime scene techies scurried around the car. Several feet away, media cameras snapped picture after picture.

"Only in New York," the newswoman said to her camera woman.

"Only in New York," the camera woman replied as she loaded a piece of equipment into the protective carrying case.

"It's a concrete jungle out here, mama" said the news reporter.

"You can say that again."

1:30 P.M.
November 7
St. Luke's Hospital

It had been a week since Autumn made her "great escape" or at least that's what the media and news was calling it. If they had an inkling of the affair between Detective Griffin and the lady cop killer, boy oh boy, he probably wouldn't be able to walk outside, let alone carry a badge. *What in the world was I thinking?* That was the question he asked him self. How did he get caught on the wrong side? It would never happen again. A new playground was being built across from Baisley Projects off of 116th and Guy R. Brewer in Queens. He planned on getting involved and making a memorial for the four kids, if only a rock with their names inscribed in it, just so that there was something in this world left behind to remember them by. He twisted in the hospital chair, which he had been camped out in for two days next to Natasha's bed side.

While he had been shot three times, his injuries were less complicated than hers. Natasha suffered a gun shot wound to her chest cavity. And her surgery didn't go so well. She went into cardiac arrest, ended up in the ICU ward where she had been in and out of consciousness for the past week until finally opening her eyes. She lay still as she regained consciousness realizing where she was and trying to remember what happened. Slowly, like pictures flickering one by one, each image reminded her of what happened.

Her hand rubbed her lower stomach, and her first thoughts were that of the baby. *Please God let my baby be okay,* she prayed.

A nurse walked over to her carrying a saline solution of liquid nutrients. "Wow, you're up. How do you feel?"

"Sore," smiled Natasha.

"Well, you took three gun shots. The whole city has been waiting for word that you're okay. You're a celebrity now," said Betty Bengals. "I kept all the newspapers for you."

"Is my baby, okay," asked Natasha.

Nurse Bengals finished hanging the solution as if she hadn't heard her question.

"Just relax, I'll get the doctor for you. You see, you got company," she said smiling at Rahjohn. "He's been sleeping in that chair now for a couple of days. I can't get him to leave."

"Tash," said Rahjohn as he slowly pulled himself out of the chair. Bandaged and wounded, it didn't matter because he was by her side, where he belonged.

"Rahjohn, is the baby okay?" she asked with tears in her eyes feeling the truth, but needing to hear it.

"Tash...I'm sorry. We lost the baby."

Natasha heard the word "we" but the word "lost" consumed her with grief.

"No, God, why?" she said as she began to cry, unable to turn her torso from him, she covered her face with her bed sheet.

"Tash, I'm so sorry," he said again, needing to hear forgiveness.

"Leave me alone," she spat, her face still buried under the sheet. She remembered following him and watching him outside Autumn's townhouse. He had been with her, the same woman that took her baby, slept with her man. The thoughts over whelmed her with grief and anger and she began to cry uncontrollably.

"Get out!" she screamed flinging the sheet from her tear-streaked face. "Get away from me! I hate you Rahjohn. How could you do that? How could you do that to me?" she screamed at him.

"Tash, please, I never meant to hurt you," said Rahjohn. "I never meant for any of this," he said bowing his head to her, barely unable to look her in the eyes.

Nurse Betty Bengals ran back over to Natasha. "Is everything okay, just calm down, you don't want to hurt yourself. Maybe it be best if you go now," she said softly to Rahjohn.

Rahjohn's eyes pleaded with her. "Tash, please, let me stay."

"For what, Rahjohn? Just go," said Natasha turning her face away from him, feeling the worse pain in her heart as tears streamed uncontrollably. She couldn't be with him, she couldn't even look at him, let alone talk to him, not after what he had done to her. For the first time in her life, she needed the window seat. Not Rahjohn, her best girlfriend, or her mama, could make her feel better at that moment. She had lost the baby, lost Rahjohn, and lost what could have been her happily ever after. Everything she had wanted had all been destroyed. And Rahjohn lost what he didn't even realize he had right in front of him, a good woman that would have held him down.

Rahjohn allowed the nurses to help him into a wheelchair and just as the nurse was rolling him away, he turned back to Natasha who was being comforted by Nurse Bengals.

"Tash, I'm so sorry."

1:31 P.M.
November 7

Autumn sat poolside at the Half Moon in Montego Bay, Jamaica. The weather was typically Caribbean in its thick heat, but tempered by the consistent, cool breezes. Her emerald green Dior two piece complemented her butter-tone skin and matched her green eyes that were hidden behind oversized Dior shades.

When it was all said and done, she walked away with close to ten million dollars, the sum total of Bacardi, Baby Wise and Biz's stashes, and did it all without revealing her hand until the very end, not even to Vita and Antoinette. They should've seen it coming, but they didn't, until it was too late.

"Damn," was all that Antoinette sighed when Autumn blew Vita's brains all over the windshield, just a second before Autumn blew her brains out too.

She sighed as if to see Autumn murder Vita made perfect sense, and in that second, resigned herself to the fact that she was about to die as well.

They had to go, in Autumn's mind, because they unlike her had been exposed. Their faces had been captured on surveillance cameras, Antoinette had been arrested, and there was no telling where they might have left an inadvertent fingerprint. Sooner or later, the police would've found them, if for no other reason than the four dead cops in Brooklyn, and then would they hold water or break under pressure? Autumn wasn't about to take that chance and so no more Vita, no more Antoinette.

A breeze tickled her body, curiously swirling along her thigh, hardening her nipples and gently kissing her neck. As it faded away, making her moan ever slightly, the sensation made her think of Rahjohn and that thought made her smile. Players were always the easiest because they thought they were doing the playing. Autumn had learned long ago that if you let a man think whatever he wanted, it was child's play to make him believe what you told him. She had used that jewel to perfection in executing her plan.

Still, she couldn't help but fantasize over their lustful episodes. She had never cum like that in her life. But then again, she thought with a giggle, she was still young and there would be others.

"Excuse me, pretty lady."

She looked up, opening her eyes to the Jamaican accent and seeing the white-coated waiter standing there.

"Yes?" she said softly.

He flashed his pearly white smile on her.

"The gentleman over there noticed that your drink is getting low and he thought you would like another," said the young Yardley as he handed her another round.

"Oh thank you," she answered, as the waiter sat a fresh mango mojito on the small table beside her, then removed the old one.

"Pretty lady, he's right over there. You can thank him yourself," the waiter smiled then walked away.

Autumn looked up, and even though she kept a poker face and a slight smirk, her heart fluttered and her adrenaline surged. Far from scared, she welcomed the challenge.

Sitting across the pool was a light brown gentleman wearing a pair of Cartier frames, a Rolex watch and a linen short set. The smile on his face was menacing but he wore the mask of civility. He raised his glass to her.

Autumn, no stranger to masks herself mentally put hers on and lifted her drink blowing him a kiss in the wind.

And so it began....

Epilogue

12:30 P.M.
April 2010

Six month's earlier at the Jade East Motel all three of them arrive in rentals one after the other and met on the backside of the motel, away from the traffic on North Conduit.

Renee Owens arranged the meeting place and was the last to enter the room.

"Damn, Antoinette, put that shit out! You gonna have me smelling like weed at work," Renee huffed.

"Aw bitch, lay down. This is a crack hotel, a muhfucka can't even smell they self in this bitch from all the crack smoke," Antoinette laughed, inhaling the blunt.

Renee sucked her teeth but didn't say anything. All her life, chicks like Antoinette had been beating her up and picking on her. She was just happy to be accepted amongst the click, even though deep down, she knew she was being used. Just like Bacardi used her for her body, her job and to stash her apartment. At least this time, she'd be getting paid for it, or so she thought.

"Okay, so the car is no problem. I hollered at him already. Spanish dude named Juan. He does all of Baby Wise's stash spots, rims, shit like that. He think he gonna get some pussy for keeping it between me and him. He gonna get a shot, alright, in the fuckin' head," Vita snickered, taking the blunt from Antoinette's extended hand.

She was by far the coldest of the crew. Ironically, though, she was a battered wifey. Vita may've been crazy, but Baby Wise was psychotic. She was well taken care of, but she paid the price in bruises. She was ready to get paid and leave some bruises of her own.

"'Nette, what's good with Face?" Autumn asked, reclining against the headboard.

Antoinette sucked her teeth, slow and arrogantly.

"Please, that nigga might as well get a ring in his nose, so I can lead him around by it. Juicy got him crazy. He ready to kidnap Michelle Obama mama if I tell him too," she bragged. Antoinette didn't mind letting the barrel spit, or even slicing anybody with the razor she kept in her mouth and flip on her tongue occasionally. But she wasn't a cold blooded killer, just a money hungry bitch.

Biz had gone against the grain, trying to turn a hoe into a housewife. But just like Face, the juicy had him crazy, too. When it came to sex, Antoinette was completely uninhibited, and would do it all, for a price.

"Okay, then we all set," Autumn nodded with satisfaction. "They ain't never gonna see it coming, especially after ya'll kidnap me. They ain't gonna suspect shit," Autumn snickered.

Suspect you, you mean, Vita thought with a sneer, but held her peace for the moment.

"Now, when bodies start dropping, there's the dude in Homicide, he's like the top detective, and no doubt in my mind, he gonna be the one assigned to the case. The best thing about it is, he hate Bacardi," Autumn explained with a smirk. "So his head is already half way to where we need it to be. I'll take it the rest of the way."

Autumn was clearly the cream of the crew, angelically

gorgeous, extremely smart and cold blooded to the core. To her, love was spelled backwards. She wasn't money hungry, but since money was the yardstick of success, she planned on measuring up.

She had masterminded the whole idea and brought all these chicks together. Antoinette and Vita had grown up in Forty Projects together. Autumn met Vita through Antoinette. She already knew Baby Wise was an abusive and possessive man, and Vita bore all the signs. It didn't take long to take Vita under her wing. With Antoinette, it took less time. The last piece of the puzzle was Renee, Bacardi and Biz's nut rag. Renee was also in a position to arrange the whole robbery, which was so vital to jump off the master plan.

"So, Halloween, right," Renee asked.

"If everything goes right, relax nay-nay girl, you'll be taken care of," Autumn said soothingly, meaning something totally different from what Renee thought.

Antoinette had to stifle a laugh. They had decided that Renee was too jittery and had to go as soon as they set things in motion. She was expendable, but to Autumn, so were Vita and Antoinette.

"That's what it is, then," Vita said, standing up and putting out the blunt. "I better get back before that nigga start wildin'."

The girls all left, heading in separate directions.

Vita pulled up on a dark block, and a man wearing a jogging sweat suit, Cartier frames and Gucci sneakers got in. It was her cousin, Fresh.

What's good, cuzzo?" he asked, kissing her on the cheek.

She winced slightly because it was still sore from when Baby Wise had backhanded her two days ago.

"Yo, that nigga still puttin' his hands on you?" he gritted.

Vita was his favorite cousin, and he was very protective of her. The only reason he hadn't killed Wise himself was because Vita had poured him a drink on the plan.

"I'ma be alright, baby, we about to make that nigga pay!"

"Yeah, just make sure I'm the one pullin' the trigger. What up, though?"

"It's all good. Like I said, it's set for Halloween."

"That's what it is then," Fresh nodded.

"But, listen Bacardi girl, Autumn," she shook her head. "I don't trust that bitch. She think she got all the fuckin' sense. I want you to keep an eye on her. She move, you move."

"Just like that?"

"Exactly."

"Say no more."

"Just be on point, when it's goin' down, I'ma text you, one word!"

He looked at her.

What's the word?"

She smiled and replied, "Masquerade."

COMMONLY ASKED QUESTIONS:

Q. **How can I find a Teri Woods book?**

A. **Order on line:**

Order an autographed book
on-line for only $10.00
www.teriwoodspublishing.com

Guaranteed Shipping within 48 hours Mon-Fri

B. **Order through the mail:**

Teri Woods Publishing
P.O. Box
Lewes, De 19958

C. **Come to Book Expos, Book Signings and Book
Events when scheduled**

Check the Teri Woods website for signing and event
schedules

D. **Call the office and order over the phone with a
major credit card.**

302-945-8085

Q. **Should I look for the body of work by Teri Woods Publishing to be in Borders or Barnes and Noble or even on Amazon?**

A. Yes, but if they don't have the book in stock, they can order it for you or you can contact the office.

Q. **I am a new book store owner and I would like to carry Teri Woods' Books. How can I do that?**

A. Contact the office, and we will supply you with lists of distributors so that you can order not only this independent line of work, but other self published authors as well.

P.S. One more time on the thank yous:

I just want to thank the many, many, people who have been there for me, helped me, touch my life and inspired me not to give up my writing. I know that this journey has taught me to appreciate many things. I've had the highest joys in my life these past years and I've had my world totally destroyed at the same time from many levels on a NY public level, which is even worse, but never have you, my fans, abandoned me or turned your backs on me. In my heart, that I know is word. I thank you and I look forward to our next coming together through the pages of one of my books. One, TW

COMING SOON

NGEL PART II-THE FINAL CHAPTER

)EADLY REIGNS-PART IV

LIBI-PART 2-NARD'S REVENGE

:ONFIDENTIAL INFORMANTS

"OR GANGSTERS ONLY

:ECRETS

ORDER FORM

Teri Woods Publishing
P.O. Box 683
Lewes, DE 19958
(302) 945-8085
www.teriwoodspublishing.com

PURCHASER INFORMATION:

NAME _____

ADDRESS_____

_____

CITY_____ STATE____ ZIP_____

PURCHASING INFORMATION:
(Please mark the books you are ordering)

TRUE TO THE GAME I   _____
TRUE TO THE GAME II   _____
TRUE TO THE GAME III   _____
B-MORE CAREFUL   _____
THE ADVENTURES GHETTO SAM   _____
DUTCH I   _____
DUTCH II   _____
DUTCH III   _____
TELL ME YOUR NAME   _____
TRIANGLE OF SINS   _____
RECTANGLE OF SINS   _____
CIRCLE OF SINS   _____
DEADLY REIGNS I   _____
DEADLY REIGNS II   _____
DEADLY REIGNS III   _____
ANGEL   _____
DOUBLE DOSE   _____
PREDATORS   _____
ALIBI   _____
BEAT THE CROSS   _____
NY'S FINEST   _____

PRICING INFORMATION:
Cost Per Book $12.41
Includes Shipping and Handling